DELIVERENCE CARTER

M. GREENFIELD

Published by Glass Spider Publishing
www.glassspiderpublishing.com

Cover by Judith S. Design & Creativity
www.judithsdesign.com

ISBN: 9781710967487
Library of Congress Control Number: 2020901995

For Kita, who is a better person than I will ever be even though she's a dog.

PROLOGUE

His home phone was ringing. Groggily, he rolled onto his side and cracked an eye. According to the digital clock on the nightstand, it was 3:05 a.m. Someone had better be dead.

The phone went silent. A few seconds later, his work cell started up and jittered across the surface of the nightstand. This could mean only one thing: someone was dead.

As a homicide detective, phone calls late at night were relatively common, though that didn't mean he had to like it. Grumbling, he reached for the phone, fumbling with it before answering.

"This is Brookes."

"Jesus, Mike! For a minute there, I didn't think you were going to pick up!"

Mike's partner, Bruce Flanagan, had always been an excitable cop, but he was a brilliant detective. The two of them had been partners since Mike transferred from Chicago last July. It had been a few months, but they were still getting used to each other.

Mike swung his legs out of bed and rubbed the back of his neck. "What's going on?"

"We've got another one," Bruce said, sounding grim.

Mike sat up straighter, now wide awake. "Same M.O.?"

"Same everything, except this time, it looks like he got a little carried away."

"Are you sure it's the same perp?"

If it was, Mike thought, that would make the third one this month alone.

"Yeah, I'm sure. You really need to get down here."

"I'm on my way."

Mike took down the address, hung up, and hunted around his messy bedroom for a pair of pants. He found them hiding under his Star Wars t-shirt featuring a faded Han Solo and Chewbacca, which he also grabbed.

He pulled the shirt over his head as he entered the kitchen and fired up the Keurig. He took his coffee into the living room, set it on the coffee table, and dropped to his knees next to the couch. It only took a few seconds of groping under the worn leather before he found his shoes, but he had the brief thought that he was a slob and his mother would be disappointed in him.

I should probably clean the house, he thought.

Mike shrugged it off. He tied his shoes, grabbed his coffee, and left the house.

***

Ogden, Utah, is a relatively small city, with a population of around 89,000, but it still has its little personal ghetto. Everything west of the train tracks was littered with drugs and abandoned buildings. It didn't take Mike long before he found the abandoned theatre Bruce had given him the address to. Bruce's black bronco was parked out front, along with a number of cop cars. Several officers were milling about the cars and CSI van.

Mike parked at the curb and got out. He brushed off the dress shirt he had added on the way over and adjusted his tie. The night was cold, and a bitter October breeze sent leaves swirling around the street. Mike pulled his jacket closed and crossed the asphalt.

Bruce was talking to one of the forensic techs. He was a big man, standing well over six feet, with a heavily tanned complexion that didn't quite go with his crew cut. He turned as Mike approached.

"Well, it's about damn time!"

"It's four in the morning. I needed coffee," Mike said. "What have we got?"

"Black female, early twenties. They think she died somewhere between eleven and one, and she was definitely killed here. A guy found her and called it in using the phone at the gas station a few blocks down, but he refused to give a name and bailed before we got there."

"Are you sure it's the same guy? The last two girls were white."

"Yeah, I know, but it might as well be the same crime scene as the other two," Bruce replied. "You'll understand when you see it."

Mike ducked beneath the crime scene tape and followed Bruce inside. They crossed through the lobby, past the bustling crowd of forensics and cops and farther into the old theatre. He passed the empty and cracked displays of the concession stands where his tired face was splintered in the reflection of the glass. Each step kicked up dust from the ragged green carpet.

Fluorescent crime scene lights were leaking into the hallway in front of theatre number one. With Bruce hot on his heels, Mike slipped a pair of protective booties over his shoes before he entered.

At first, the lighting made it difficult to see. Mike brought a palm up against the glare. Squinting in the shadow of his hand, Mike could see the body where it lay broken beneath the torn fabric of the old projector screen. He walked down the aisle, past the old, worn chairs, eyes fixed on the slaughtered body of the young woman. He walked around the right side of the stage, trotted up the stairs, and stopped where the blood began.

With a slow and calculating look, his eyes swept the stage. He took in the blood that pooled around the body; watched the way it glittered and how the edges puckered with a thin meniscus.

It was fresh, probably only a few hours old. Long enough to have started drying but recent enough to shine.

Mike stared at the projector screen as he absorbed the pattern created by the arcs of blood that had been splashed across its surface. The screen was little more than a dry piece of fabric, and it had sucked in the violence without a single run. It preserved the blood splatter in a pristine fashion.

Finally, his gaze settled on the woman's body. She had been split from throat to groin, the muscle and ribs peeled back to reveal her internal organs, which the killer had removed and arranged on the stage around her.

Mike moved around the body, making sure to give it a wide berth so he wouldn't disturb any of the evidence. He crouched near her head to get a better look at her face.

Her eyes were swollen closed. Her nose was crushed, and her mouth hung slack to reveal the emptiness where there should have been a tongue.

Bruce's voice broke Mike's focus. "What do you think?" he asked from behind Mike.

Mike shook his head and sighed. "I would say this has a lot of similarities to the other two victims. They both had parts of their faces removed, but they were all external, like eyes and ears. All have been young women found around this area, and all of them have been opened up. But the other killings were clean, almost surgical. This? This is different." He stood and faced Bruce. "This woman was beaten, something we didn't see with the other two. That tells me he's escalating. Was she chloroformed?"

"We'll have to wait for the toxicology report to know for sure," Bruce said.

Mike nodded and stroked his chin in a very Sherlock Holmes manner. "Maybe she was, and it wore off," he speculated. "She woke up, maybe fought him or said something he didn't like, so he flipped out, cut out her tongue, and beat her. When killers slip like this, they usually leave something behind. Did Forensics find anything?"

"Forensics finds lots of useful things," said a woman's voice.

Mike turned to face her.

It was Samantha Jenkins. She was a forensic technician who was very good at her job and knew it. She was tall and beautiful, with thick black hair framing her teak skin and narrow, dark eyes that regarded him above high cheekbones. Her sharp chin held a slight elevation that suggested offense. She held a heavy duffle bag and cast Mike an indignant look.

"Doubting my abilities?" she asked sarcastically.

Mike smiled despite himself. "Wouldn't dream of it."

Samantha seemed pleased with his answer and gave him a small smile in return. "We haven't found anything that would be immediately useful yet," she said. "No fingerprints, and so far, all the blood around here seems to be from the victim. We'll know more when we get all this back to the lab."

"Thank you, Sam," Mike replied.

Samantha gave him a nod before moving away.

"Damn it," Mike said once she was out of earshot.

That made three crime scenes with no fingerprints and no DNA.

Bruce was watching Samantha go, ignoring Mike's curse. "So," Bruce said, "how long have you two been bangin'?"

Mike threw his partner a withering look. "Has anyone found the victim's personal belongings?"

"Nope. Taken, just like the others."

"This guy is making things really difficult," Mike growled.

"Don't worry, we'll catch him," Bruce replied. He was practically glowing with energy.

Bruce had definitely found his calling in life, but Mike was a little more reserved as he looked at the body of the slaughtered woman.

"Yeah," Mike sighed, "I guess we will."

CHAPTER 1
EVERYDAY ZOMBIE

Sometimes things just wander into your life with the intent to fuck you up forever. They can be all kinds of things: a horrible relationship, the death of someone near to you, mortgages, marriages, taxes, whatever. My name is Deliverence Carter, spelled with an "e," and being a zombie has done that to me.

I know—not the most common thing to bump into, but it isn't anything like a *World War Z* remake. I'm not completely raving mad, nor am I slow and idiotic while I wander around searching for my next meal. I'm just a normal woman (as far as my conservative mother is concerned) who happens to eat brains when the occasion calls for it.

In fact, the whole zombie thing is quite new to me. I have only been a member of the undead for the past three years. Three years that have been a constant dance between human normalcy and my ravenous cravings. Despite this, I have done my best to keep my secret a secret.

Working as a professional dog groomer makes that goal easier since all of my clients are animals and all of their owners just think

I'm a little weird. This is fine with me. I suppose I *am* a little weird.

Today, I was working my way through a soapy bath with a standard poodle named Clarence. He was a regular customer of mine but didn't like his baths, no matter how many times he came. Whenever I had an appointment with Clarence, I could guarantee I was going to be just as soapy and wet as him. So there I was, dressed in my black apron that was doing nothing to stop the onslaught of water. My proudly bred Irish mane of curly red hair was pulled back in a messy bun, and tiny sudsy strands were stuck to my forehead.

"Okay, Clarence," I said as he wiggled around in the tub, "how about a rinse?"

I scooped the loose hair from the bottom of the tub, watching as the water spiraled down the drain. Clarence barked and made an attempt to escape but was caught by his leash and held in place. He cast the leash, and then me, a scathing look.

I raised my hands. "This isn't my fault."

I pulled down the showerhead and tested the temperature of the water before rinsing his silky coat. I was massaging the shampoo out of his curls when I felt him shudder under my touch.

Clarence jerked his head and stared at the door leading to the reception area. I followed his gaze, glancing through the large windows that looked out to the reception desk and waiting room. I knew better than to ignore animals, especially now that primal instinct was something we shared.

As Clarence bounced nervously in the tub, my eyes fell on a mother and small boy who were sitting in the waiting room. She was reading a magazine, but the boy looked pale, maybe even a little scared, as he sat with his hands folded in his lap, his gaze focused on the floor.

I narrowed my eyes suspiciously. I looked back at the mother and then around the waiting room as I continued rinsing Clarence, but I didn't see anything out of the ordinary in the shop. I turned the water off but continued to watch the waiting room as I replaced the shower head and pumped conditioner into my hand. I worked it into Clarence's shiny coat with my fingers without needing to look. I could wash a dog in my sleep.

Finally, I saw it. I call them Minchkins—kind of like a play on Munchkins, but a hell of a lot creepier. They like to take the form of children, perhaps because the veil of innocence is so much more disturbing. They enjoy death and destruction and feed off of fear, especially that of children that can feel or see them. I think they target the young because kids feel every emotion so purely. They haven't yet experienced life, which teaches you to mix and dull your feelings.

Minchkins have been a part of my life since becoming a zombie, though luckily not very often. I figure since I am now something in-between living and dead, it gives me the ability to experience things humans can't. Such as Minchkins. And here one was, rising out of the floor like black ink.

I watched it take the form of a filthy little girl dressed in rags. Her hair was a matted mess that fell across her pale face, soulless eyes fixed on the little boy.

Under my hands, Clarence shuddered. His eyes darted about but never focused on the Minchkin. He could feel her presence, but he couldn't see her.

I could, however, and I watched grimly as she slinked across the room toward the boy. Her face stretched and contorted, forcing her facial features to roll onto the back of her head as her mouth became a gaping, black void. The Minchkin's large, black eyes glinted as she swallowed the boy's face.

Of course, only *I* stood witness to this horror. A moment later, the Minchkin stepped back, and her face returned to normal. She giggled a harsh and chilling child's giggle you hear in horror movies. It seemed far too loud, echoing through the salon without the hindrance of walls or doors to silence its paranormal sound.

Clarence began to really struggle now. He whined and pulled against the leash that kept him anchored to the front of the tub.

"Shh," I told him gently, "it's alright, you're fine."

But his discomfort had attracted the nasty little devil's attention. She slid through the wood of the door as if it weren't there at all and glided across the floor toward us.

I fixed my eyes on Clarence as I worked the conditioner into his coat. I was determined not to let the Minchkin know I could see her. She stopped close enough to me that I could have reached out and touched her, and her face began to contort.

The little bitch is going to feed off of Clarence, I realized. *Well, not if I can help it.*

Whistling cheerily, I sidestepped into her and made it a point not to smirk when she slid away with a hiss and a glower. Minchkins, for whatever reason, didn't like to be touched, and though walking into her was anything but comfortable for me, it accomplished my goal. She slipped away from the tub and Clarence. I rinsed out his coat, shut off the water, and untied his leash.

"C'mon," I said, "let's get you dry."

Clarence hopped out of the tub hurriedly and trotted after me to the grooming tables, where Clara was trimming a Pomeranian. The Minchkin trailed after us like an oozing shadow. Obediently, Clarence hopped onto the table. He liked this part, probably because it meant his grooming was almost over.

I flipped on the blow dryer, blasting water out of his coat as I worked a comb through his curls. The Minchkin came to stand at the head of the table and was watching me with a scowl that sent chills down my spine. She was now completely uninterested in anyone else; Clara and the dogs might as well have not existed.

I sighed as I fluffed Clarence's coat. Sometimes, I miss being human and not having to see all the lovely things being dead shows you. Of course, it isn't all bad. As a zombie, I am impervious to almost any kind of harm. I'm stronger and faster than I was, and sometimes the ghosts and spirits I encounter are friendly. Lonely, maybe, but friendly. It's just the days when I have to see the angry ones—the Minchkins, the poltergeists, or the horrible deaths of innocent people—that it becomes hard. Not to mention the occasional need to eat someone.

I turned the dryer down and aimed it above Clarence's head so it blew down over his forehead and the top of his nose. He closed his eyes against the blast and tilted his face upward. Clarence was one of the few dogs I groomed that liked the blow dryer. I flipped the dryer off and went to work on his face. Gently, I brought the comb through the hair on his ears, being careful to brace it with my fingers as to not pull too hard.

"Del?" Clara asked.

Looking at Clara forced me to look past the Minchkin. I made it a point to look over its head. "Yes?"

Clara had paused in her work to watch me with assessing eyes and a furrowed brow. Clara was one of those short, curvy girls, the kind with really large hips and breasts but not a lot of waist. She was a pretty, flamboyant woman straight from the heart of Ogden's ghetto, with perfect olive skin and thick, curly black hair she kept in a braid at work. Her face was exotic, with full lips and large but narrow black eyes. Calculating eyes that were watching me intently.

"I'm fine," I said before she could ask me anything.

Clara doesn't know what I am. She is my coworker but also my friend, and I want to keep it that way. This makes little zombie pep talks out of the question. However, Clara is aware that I am rather strange and chalks it up to psychic intuition. This is something I am willing to allow her to think, since it gives me a way to vent about some of the strange things that happen to me on an almost daily basis.

Clara nodded and didn't ask anything else as she tied a bow into the tan fur of the Pomeranian, but I knew it would come up later. It always did. Clara is one of those bullheaded, intelligent, and stubborn people who gets an idea into her head and there is no going back. It doesn't help that most of the time, she's right.

She set the dog down on the floor, snapped a leash onto her collar, and walked her out to the waiting room where she could be rescued from the terror of the groomers for another two weeks.

The Minchkin followed, abruptly losing interest in Clarence and me to trail after Clara, who was now ringing the mother and son up at the counter. The Minchkin held the poor boy's hand, stroking his hair with the other. She gazed at him with a longing that made me sick as her face stretched and reformed repeatedly.

I knew this could only mean one thing. The little boy was going to die, and soon, or the Minchkin wouldn't hold so much interest in him. Her excitement made me certain it was going to be a horrible, gruesome death.

I chewed my lip nervously. I had no way of knowing when something was going to happen, only that it was going to be relatively soon. Probably within the next few days. There had to be something I could do. He couldn't be much older than eight.

The boy's mother was signing the receipt. I was running out of time to make a decision. The two of them left the salon, and Clara returned to the back room.

"Clara, I need you to finish Clarence. He's almost done." I untied my apron and tossed it into the dirty clothes hamper.

"Where're you goin'?" she asked as she took up the blow dryer.

"There's something I have to do. I'll explain later."

I pushed through the door to the waiting room and hurried out to the street. The boy and his mother were nowhere to be seen.

"Shit," I muttered. I turned around on the busy sidewalk. "Shit!"

On my third spin, I spotted them getting into a car a block up from me. The boy was getting into the back seat while the Minchkin fluttered around him like a gruesome insect. Suddenly, she froze. The boy closed his door, and the car motored away. The Minchkin remained motionless.

Slowly, her head swiveled independently of her body until her dark eyes settled on me. I avoided looking directly at her, instead looking past her, but I could see her clearly as she began skipping backward down the street—skipping straight through oncoming cars.

Someone touched my shoulder, causing me to yelp and spin in surprise.

"I'm sorry," a familiar voice said, "I wasn't trying to startle you."

It was Adrian Keller, the man who had the power to make me weak at the knees with a glance. A fact I hid with great dignity, except maybe from Clara. He wasn't much taller than me, maybe five-ten to my five-seven, but he was imposing with a muscular build and piercing chocolate eyes.

Being under his scrutiny always gave me the sensation he was looking through me. It was an unsettling feeling, which is why, as much as I was attracted to him, I tried to avoid him. Something that was made difficult considering I saw him every other Tuesday at 9 o'clock.

"Um, it's fine," I said quickly. "Are you on your way to pick up Clarence?"

Halfway across the street, the Minchkin paused as she considered the two of us. She glanced from Adrian to me several times before twisting her head the right way around and sinking into the ground, vanishing instantly.

"Yes." Adrian arched a well-groomed eyebrow as he took in my flustered appearance. "Are you okay?"

"Totally fine, thanks." I looked down the street as the mother and son duo took a right turn and disappeared. "Shit," I muttered.

Adrian followed my gaze. "Someone you know?"

"No," I said unconvincingly. "Well, I mean, yes. They're clients at the shop. They, uh, forgot their receipt."

Adrian gave me a bemused smile that told me in no uncertain terms he didn't believe me, but he didn't see a reason to push it. We seemed to reach a sort of silent agreement and started toward the shop together. We were about halfway there when Adrian broke the silence.

"How about dinner?"

I stumbled. "Dinner? Tonight?"

He chuckled. "Is that too short notice?"

"I, uh, shouldn't. I'm supposed to go see my mom."

Adrian held the door open for me politely. "Maybe another time, then."

"Maybe. I'll have Clara check you out."

I shuffled past him quickly and pushed through the door to the back. Immediately, I felt like an idiot. I had all but run from him.

Clara was combing out a rough collie, and Clarence could be seen looking indignant but pristinely groomed in the kennels behind her.

"That was quick," she said.

I shrugged. "I saw a Minchkin, but I lost it."

"Anything else?" she pressed.

"I bumped into Adrian, but the Minchkin bailed when he showed up."

Clara was grinning at me.

"What?" I demanded.

"Adrian Keller, huh? How'd that go?"

"I'm talking about a Minchkin following a little boy around to watch his death, and you want to know how bumping into Adrian Keller went?" I asked in disbelief.

"Listen, girl, I can't see all the heebie-jeebie shit you can, so I don't bother myself with worryin' about it. Besides, you said the Minchkin ditched." Clara paused to pick a knot out of the collie's coat with her straight comb. "So, I want to know what it was like to bump into mister tall, dark, and handsome."

"He's not *that* tall," I said lamely. "He invited me to dinner."

"Get him, girl!" Clara exclaimed.

"I told him no. I said that I had to see my mom."

"Liar, liar, pants on fire. What in the hell is the matter with you? You could be goin' to dinner with the sexiest client we have, and you're goin' to chicken out?"

"There is nothing wrong with not wanting to go out with a man that makes me forget my brain. I feel like such an idiot around him," I snapped.

"That's called attraction," Clara shot back, "and that sensation is common sense leavin' your body."

"Will you just go check him out? I didn't ask for your opinion on this," I growled.

She smiled. "No one ever does."

CHAPTER 2
THE VISION

Later that night, I stood holding a paper grocery bag, trying to jam my key into my apartment deadbolt. Finally, after a long, obnoxious struggle, I got the key into the lock and the bolt slid back with a reluctant *thunk*. I turned the knob, and the door swung open into the silence of my apartment. Within, the hallway was dark, and the carpet muffled my footsteps as I entered.

I was immediately suspicious. Stephen, my roommate, was never quiet unless he was up to something. It was like living with a toddler. A six-foot-five, flamboyant toddler.

"Stephen?" I called.

No one answered, but I wasn't convinced. He was always home by now, and who knew what he could be up to? With Stephen, nothing was out of the question.

I crossed the living room and proceeded into the kitchen, where I found Stephen standing in front of the stove, stark naked with his back to me. He hadn't heard me due to the earbuds connected to the iPod on his armband. He was cooking something, and I guessed it was eggs. Eggs were one of his favorite things.

"Stephen," I said, unphased by his nudity. I caught him naked often. "Stephen!"

He jumped and ripped out his earbuds as he spun to face me, strategically blocking any view of his groin with the spatula. "Oh! Del! I didn't think you would be home yet."

I shook my head. "Stephen, you're naked."

"Yes, Del, yes, I am." He turned, flipped the eggs, replaced the spatula, and faced me again.

"Stephen," I sighed, "we've talked about this."

"I know!" he protested. "And you weren't home until just now! After Carl left . . . you must have just missed him . . . I was hungry. So I came out here." He turned to flip the eggs onto a plate. "And then POOF, here you are. I've been out here maybe five minutes. Jesus, do you watch through the windows so you can catch me naked? You're terrible."

I sighed and rolled my eyes, smiling at the ceiling. "Where are your clothes?"

"Everywhere," was his reply. "Actually, I'm surprised you didn't see my shirt, 'cause I'm pretty sure it's in the living room."

I put the grocery bag on the counter and left on a quest to find Stephen's clothes. I returned a moment later with the pants I found in the hallway, which I had miraculously managed not to trip over before.

Stephen was now perched on the counter. There was a dish towel with a rooster on the front draped over his lap as he devoured his eggs over easy on toast.

I looked at the towel and wondered if the design had been on purpose. When I looked up, I found Stephen smirking at me.

The design had been on purpose.

I handed him his pants and turned around as he hopped off the counter to get into them.

"So, who's Carl?" I asked.

"The flavor of the week. Do you like my hair?"

Stephen had added hot-pink streaks to his naturally pitch-black hair. Sometimes I thought Stephen's gaydom was so cliché it was funny, but I never told him so.

"I love the hair," I said.

It was true. The hair was fabulous.

Stephen beamed. "I brought you dinner. It's in the fridge." He took his eggs and toast to the small table we had tucked into the corner of the kitchen and sat down.

I opened the fridge and stared in at the small Tupperware container on the top shelf. Inside, the frontal lobe of some poor deceased person was clearly visible. With an inner sigh, I picked up the container and got a fork, grabbed some pepper from above the microwave, and sat across from Stephen.

I popped the lid and shook some pepper flakes over the pinkish-grey brain matter. I stabbed my fork into the mass and squished it around before digging in. Stephen was already halfway through his eggs, totally unperturbed by my gruesome display.

As I am sure you have deduced by now, Stephen knows what I am. He has been my steady supply of brains since becoming my roommate and knows about my condition all too well. Lucky for me, he thinks it's fascinating.

Stephen has a thing for the color pink, men, and the macabre. Working as a medical examiner will do that to you. He's been an M.E. for a little over five years and works for the local hospital. He brings me brains on a regular basis due to his access to any number of bodies. Since he also does the paperwork, any "missing material" simply isn't logged.

He isn't just my supplier, he is my friend, and living with him is surprisingly easy.

"So," I said, "what's the deal with Carl?"

Stephen shrugged. "I suppose we'll see. Honestly, I'm not holding out for anything. He seems like the type that would want to go somewhere, and I just don't have time for a relationship. They're so tedious." Suddenly, he was glowering. "But enough about me. Clara called. You've been holding out on me."

Oh, the problems of having friends who are friends.

"I don't know what you're talking about," I lied.

"Don't bullshit me. Clara told me you had a chance at dinner with Adrian Keller."

"Nope."

"And you turned him down!"

"I'm not talking about this." I slapped the lid on my brains and made a run for it, barely making it into my bedroom in time to lock Stephen out. I could hear him in the hallway as he paced and ranted about never knowing what a date with Adrian Keller would be like.

"You're sucking the fun out of everything!" he yelled through the bedroom door. "How am I supposed to live vicariously through you if you won't go on a date with him?!"

From within the safety of my room, I set my brains on the nightstand and plopped on the edge of my bed, cracking a smile. Stephen had had a crush on Adrian for as long as I had, and maybe even longer. Stephen had been friends with Clara for years, and Adrian had been her client long before becoming mine. I really had no idea how long Stephen had been chasing after Adrian, but I did know it was hilarious.

With a grunt, I pulled my shoes off and wiggled my toes in the plush carpet. I leaned back on my hands and looked around the room. It was dark, and what little light leaked in from the windows cast eerie shadows across the walls and ceiling.

CRASH!

I bolted upright and stared around the room as I tried to locate the source of the noise. My eyes fell on the fire escape outside my window.

There was another loud clang of metal against metal as I approached the window and quietly flipped the latch. I slid the pane up just far enough to duck through and stepped out onto the fire escape.

The fire escape was on the back of my apartment, overlooking the parking lot. I had a clear view of the cars and dumpsters where old Mr. Santiago was loudly throwing out his trash. He had three bags on the pavement around him, and just as I looked, he heaved one over the lip of the dumpster. It made a spectacular crash as it hit the bottom. He noticed me staring and glared at me, waving his cane.

I raised my hands in submission and ducked back into my bedroom. I gave him a few minutes, then I returned to the fire escape with my brains in tow. I slid the window closed behind me and leaned on the railing, my fork buried in Frontal Lobe Supreme.

The fire escape didn't offer an overly scenic view, but I didn't mind. I stared past the now vacant parking lot to the street. It was getting late, somewhere around eleven o'clock, so I was surprised when I saw a thin figure enter the lot. She walked down the aisle between the cars, her gait swift but not overly hurried.

For a moment, I thought she was a new tenant. I was certain I had never seen her before. She was of medium height, with slender shoulders and waist, and she wore a pale-blue sundress that fell just short of her knees. It looked too cold to be worn in the middle of October.

As she came nearer, I could see that she was African American. Halfway across the lot, she looked up and saw me watching her. I raised my hand to wave, and she stopped abruptly, staring at me.

That was when I knew the truth.

She was dead.

As if my realization had jolted the illusion of her life, I saw her for what she was: a ghost. A trapped soul. Standing in the parking lot below me, her facade fell away.

Bruises slowly engulfed her face. Her nose broke itself and was smashed to one side while first one eye and then the other swelled shut above it.

Blood ran from between her lips and down her neck, cascading onto her dress. Where the crimson tide touched it, the dress melted away, leaving her in the nude.

Abruptly, her chest split open, and the skin peeled itself back as the bone of her sternum broke with an audible snap. The fissure continued to her pelvis, leaving all of her internal organs exposed. Then, as though gravity had suddenly called to them, they tumbled from her body and splattered upon the pavement around her, leaving her torso gaping open like the eyes she could no longer use.

"Oh, my God," I whispered as I bore witness to the horror of what someone had done to her.

Instantly, she was once again the young and beautiful woman in the pale-blue summer dress, watching me. Tears pooled in her large brown eyes and rolled down her cheeks.

We stood there for a moment in silence, watching each other. I looked down at the brain I had been eating. I knew it had been hers, and it had been her murder that I'd had the pleasure of viewing.

When I glanced back up, she was gone. I placed the container on the fire escape and braced myself against the railing.

I knew what came next.

***

"Mindi, c'mon, have another drink."

I turned and looked at the woman sitting at the bar beside me, and I knew her name was Jessica. She was holding out a shot glass.

25

"No thanks," I said, too drunk to properly focus on her face. "I think I've had enough. I should go home."

I fought the urge to vomit with some deep breathing, sliding my stool back from the bench and standing.

"Are you okay?" Jessica asked worriedly. "I can call you an Uber."

I waved her off. "Nope. I'll just walk home. Call you tomorrow?"

Jessica smiled. "Of course. Love ya, girl."

Her final words faded out, echoing as though they had been shouted down a long corridor: "Girl . . . girl . . . girl . . ."

Standing on the sidewalk outside the bar, I stared up at the neon sign that was far too hard for me to read. The Shack swirled in and out of focus.

"Jesus, I'm hammered," I mumbled out loud.

I shook my head and staggered down the sidewalk. Occasionally, I stopped to catch my balance and focus hard on not launching the contents of my stomach into the street. My head was spinning, and the world around me was swirling. Just putting one foot in front of the other might as well have been running a marathon.

I was faintly aware as a van passed me and stopped at the curb. I was watching my feet intently, focusing on the sidewalk, when there came the sound of pounding footsteps. Huge hands grabbed me roughly—one wrapped around my arm, and the other pressed a rag to my face.

A harsh chemical burned my nose, causing me to panic. Angrily, violently, I lashed out at my attacker, driving my elbow behind me as I flailed and stomped.

I was determined to hurt him, to get away, and I fought him with everything I had. He grunted from the impact of my blows and loosened his grip just enough for me to wrench myself free.

I stumbled, fell to my knees, and pulled myself back to my feet. I could feel the effects of the chemical weighing heavily on my limbs.

I staggered.

Maybe if I could just make it a little farther . . .

The ground rushed up to meet me as I collapsed into the grass beside the sidewalk. I wanted to stand, to run, to do *anything* . . . but instead, I slipped away into darkness.

***

I came to slowly. Confused, cold, and in pain.

My eyes fluttered open, and a massive yellowed cloth came into focus. I stared at the texture of it, fixating on the aging hue and the roughness of the fabric.

Is that a projector screen?

Distantly, I became aware that I was naked, though I couldn't remember how I got that way.

Where am I?

I fought to turn my head. It was so heavy that it might as well have been glued to the hard floor beneath me. Every movement was tortured and slow. So painfully slow.

I was awakening to the fact there was something terribly wrong with my chest, and possibly my stomach.

I urged my arms to move—for anything to move. The fingers on my right hand curled from the effort, and I dragged my arm across the floor's wooden surface. Shaking and weary, my hand touched my waist and came away bloody. A dark viscous liquid coated my palm and rolled down my arm in bloody tendrils.

Shocked and disgusted, I hardly felt it when my arm fell to the stage with a thud. Horribly disoriented, I fought to comprehend my situation.

What happened? What is wrong?

One word cut through the fog that threatened my consciousness: escape. I knew I had to escape.

But I was so heavy. I was so cold.

Faintly, a door opened, then closed. There was enraged yelling and the thundering of footsteps on old stairs above my head. I tried to make words come, to plead for help or mercy, but my breath rattled out of my throat as a pained whisper.

A fist slammed into my face. Once, and then what could have been a hundred more times. My nose shattered. Blood burst hot and wet across my face. Tears blurred my vision, and somewhere I found the strength to scream.

My assailant was screaming too. For me to shut up. Threatening further violence.

I didn't care. I screamed until my throat was hoarse and a large bloodied hand reached into my mouth, pulled out my tongue, and sliced it away.

Blood gushed. My shrieks turned to gurgles. I was choking, coughing, spitting, drowning in my own blood.

Behind me, I could hear manic laughter. There was a sharp, ripping pain in my chest. I stared up at the shadows flitting across the old, tattered projection screen and watched them dance to the music of my death.

***

I jerked abruptly as the vision ended, whacking my head on the fire escape. I held the railing in a white-knuckled grip as I sat crumpled in the corner. I sucked in huge, chest-wracking gulps of air and struggled to shake off the sensation of choking.

It was always hard for me to experience someone else's death. There was simply no way to prepare myself for feeling someone die. It never got easier, and I doubted it ever would. I sat against the wall of my apartment building, sweaty and shaking with the sound of Mindi's screams echoing in my ears.

The painful burn of tears welled and fell down my face.

"I am so sorry," I whispered into the night, for naturally, there was no one there to hear me.

I pulled my knees up to my chest and wrapped my arms tightly around them, rocking slightly as I watched the place where I had seen Mindi. She wasn't there. Her appearance had only been the precursor to my vision.

The tears streamed, and I let them. I hadn't been expecting something so cruel, something so disgustingly evil. But there was another emotion mingling with the sadness.

Rage. Deep, unadulterated rage. Rage I had only ever known since becoming a zombie. The kind of anger that leaves you cold and prepared.

Quietly, my sorrow was washed away in a swell of anger. I gripped the railing tightly and pulled myself up.

Someone was going to pay.

CHAPTER 3
AN UNEXPECTED
ENCOUNTER

The day after my vision of Mindi's death was my day off. Call it fate, call it luck, whatever you want. Being a zombie and therefore a member of the undead, I don't have to sleep, but I like to. Even when I don't, I love to lay in bed in a sort of daze that has a lot of the same effect. Unfortunately, none of that happened, due to the disturbing level of my experience the night before.

It was seven when I decided to throw in the towel and rolled out of bed, literally. I flopped onto my hands and knees. I thumped my head once on the carpet, groaned, and dragged myself to my feet.

I pulled on a pair of pants through the haze of half-opened eyes and snapped my bra behind my back by muscle memory alone. I yanked a shirt over my head and stumbled into the hallway, leaning heavily on the wall on my way to the kitchen. The smell of coffee was permeating the apartment, beckoning to me as I entered. Stephen was sitting at the kitchen table, reading a fashion magazine with a cup of coffee in his hand.

"Good morning!" he chirped without looking up.

I meant to reply with a good morning of my own, but all that came out were a series of growls.

Needless to say, I am not a morning person.

Stephen glanced up at me as I headed for the coffee pot and chuckled. "Honey, you look like shit. Do you know that your shirt is on inside out? I think it might be backwards, too. It's hard to tell with those t-shirts you love to wear."

I whipped my shirt off, corrected it, and pulled it back over my head. I had done it without thinking. Now it sank in that I had just flashed my roommate. Well, I figured, it was too late to be embarrassed. Besides, I caught Stephen naked around the apartment all the time.

I poured myself a cup of coffee and sat across from Stephen. I snatched the magazine from his hand.

"What have I told you about bringing home murder victims?" I growled.

Stephen arched a cynical eyebrow, his expression cold. "The cause of death hadn't been determined yet."

"She was disemboweled," I said. "People don't accidentally get disemboweled."

"It was either her or an elderly gentleman that had Alzheimer's," Stephen replied. "We couldn't have you wandering off forgetting your name and where you live, now, could we?"

Still brooding, I clutched my coffee mug with both hands. "When was she brought in?"

"Early yesterday morning. I looked her over then, but I haven't filed all of my paperwork yet. The cause of death can't be determined without the toxicology report, but I'm betting asphyxiation. Her lungs were full of blood, probably from when her tongue was removed." Stephen was watching me closely now, clearly wanting to know what I had seen.

"She was awake when he cut her tongue out," I said flatly. "She experienced the entire thing. It was fucking horrible."

"He?" Stephen pressed.

"Yeah. There was someone yelling, and it was a man's voice, and when he grabbed her, he was really big."

"Anything else?"

"Where's The Shack?" I asked. "It's a bar."

"Haven't the slightest idea. I'm certainly not drinking anywhere called The Shack."

"She was kidnapped from right around there." I pulled out my phone and opened the Google browser. "Where was her body found? It looked like an old theatre."

Stephen shrugged. "I'll have to see what I can find out. Did she have a name in your vision?"

I searched for The Shack in Ogden, Utah. I received two results. "Mindi," I said. "I didn't get a last name."

"Well, I'm going in soon. Maybe you could come by? It might trigger some more visions."

"Maybe. Right now, I have a bar and a building with a projector screen to hunt down."

***

Mike sat in the parking lot of the Ogden City morgue. It was a large building across the street from Ogden Memorial Hospital, and it was where the body of Jane Doe had been brought. He flipped through the thin case file without really reading anything. On the passenger seat beside him were his notes from the other two victims, tucked away in manila envelopes.

This was the third victim in as many weeks, and he was beginning to feel the pressure. Ogden was on edge. Everyone was suspicious. Everyone wanted the killer found, and they wanted them found *right now*. Even the mayor had called him.

With a sigh, Mike put away his notes in the folder marked J. Doe and set it on the seat with the others. He opened his door, switched the engine off, and headed into the morgue.

Stephen Hopkins was the attendant on duty. Mike had met him before, and as usual, he was flitting around the dead bodies like a butterfly around flowers. He was a tall man with black hair that sported hot-pink highlights, and his lab coat made him look lankier than he was.

Although Mike had never had any issues with Stephen, he didn't like him. He felt Stephen was too flamboyant.

"Hello, Detective!" Stephen greeted him cheerily. "What can I do for you?"

Mike tried not to stare at the hair. He was only marginally successful. "I know this is probably unrealistic, but I was wondering if the toxicology report is back?"

Stephen arched an eyebrow. "I only got the samples sent in last night. I haven't seen a report."

Mike pinched the bridge of his nose and sighed. "Thanks anyway. Will you let me know when you have it?"

"You'll be my first call. I'll see if I can pull some strings and get it done sooner. Out of curiosity, where was she found?"

Mike fixed Stephen with the cop stare. "Why?"

"There were wood splinters in her hair," Stephen said coolly. "They were coated in black paint."

"You know I'm not supposed to divulge any information about the case to you."

Stephen held up his hand. "Scout's honor, I won't tell a living soul."

Mike sighed. It was going to be a long day.

***

I stood just outside the crime scene tape and stared up at the old theatre, flashlight in hand. Stephen had called me an hour before and said he had managed to get it out of one of the detectives working the case that Mindi had been found in an old theatre. A couple of internet searches later, and here I was.

I wasn't supposed to go past the crime scene tape. But this wasn't the first time—or the last time—I would be sneaking into a crime scene. I knew any evidence would have already been collected. I also knew the scene was deserted. I rubbed my hands on my thighs to relieve my anxiety, ducked under the tape, and headed in.

The only light inside came from the broken windows, and to say the place had an eerie ambiance would be a gross understatement.

I flipped the switch on my flashlight and cast the beam onto the floor of the theatre. Scuffle marks across the dusty carpet marked the parade of people that had come and gone from theatre number one. I pushed through the swinging door, and the beam of my flashlight fell on the now deserted stage.

For a moment, there was the sound of voices, the light of the projector against the screen, a sea of turned heads facing the movie that had happened so long ago. To my left, a child ran down the aisle . . .

The scene was gone. The theatre was once again abandoned, and my flashlight the only illumination. Ahead of me, the stained projector screen loomed ominously. I trotted up the stairs but kept my distance from the middle of the stage where Mindi's body had been.

I was wrenched into a memory that wasn't mine. There was the sound of an engine, the feeling of motion, exhaust in my nose.

Where was I? A van?

The sound of a door opening jarred me from my vision. I spun to see a man entering the theatre, looking just as shocked by my presence as I was by his.

***

Mike stopped dead in the entrance and stared at the woman standing on the stage. She was holding a flashlight, her eyes wide with surprise.

It was Mike who broke the silence. "What the hell do you think you're doing here? This is a crime scene! I could arrest you!"

"What are you, a cop?" Del asked. She hopped off the stage and started up the aisle.

"Detective Michael Brookes, Homicide," Mike said. He pulled his leather wallet out of his jacket and flipped it open to show her the metal inside. "Would you care to explain what you're doing here?"

"Exploring."

"Exploring? Does crime scene tape mean nothing to you?"

***

I watched the detective carefully and tried not to fidget. Cops always make me nervous.

I had never seen him before, which made me wonder if he was new. Because of my friendship with Stephen, I knew just about everyone on the force. He was tall with a lanky build and taut shoulders. He had sandy-brown hair and pale eyes that watched me with suspicion. The bags under his eyes and the shadow on his chin told me he didn't sleep enough, but altogether he was a good-looking guy.

"I didn't see any tape," I said. "I came in through the back."

He watched me for a moment while I wondered where exactly the back was and if there was, indeed, caution tape there. I knew he wasn't buying my story; I could see it in his expression. He flipped out a notepad and pulled a pen from his pocket. "What's your name?"

I glanced at the pad. *Shit.*

"Deliverence Carter," I said, and waited. This wasn't the first murder investigation I had been tied up with, and sometimes my name could give me trouble with the force, but he just wrote it down.

"It's spelled with an e," I said. I couldn't help myself.

"Okay, Miss Carter. I am going to pretend that I didn't see you here as long as you get out and *stay* out."

I nodded, and he followed me out of the theatre. He stood on the curb to make sure I was walking away, then turned and went back to the movies.

CHAPTER 4
IN WHICH A DATE GOES AWRY

I crouched behind a dying hedge across from the theatre and waited for my unexpected visitor to leave so I could slip back in and hopefully pick up another vision.

After two hours, there was still no sign of him leaving. His black Lincoln sat stoically at the curb, the sun glinting off the windows.

"Shit," I muttered.

What the hell could he be doing in there? My legs were cramped, and my left foot was asleep. I had twigs and a few leaves in my hair and probably looked like the wild woman of Borneo.

With a grunt, I stood and resolved to return another time. I stomped some of the life back into my foot and started down the street to where I had parked my red VW Bug—an older model dating back to when they still had character.

I was unlocking the door when the wave of hunger hit me. My vision blurred, and I leaned heavily on the doorframe. Then came the all too familiar pounding behind eyes I knew were turning crimson. My mouth went dry, and an overwhelming urge to kill filled me.

My gaze shifted to the theatre down the street, where I knew a quite vulnerable human waited.

I shook my head violently to clear the thoughts that threatened to steal my humanity. After a few heavy drawn-out breaths, I climbed into my car and roared away.

The city morgue had limited access for a number of obvious reasons, but there was a small callbox next to the door where you could page to be let in. Being a close friend and roommate with the lead medical examiner, I knew the buzzer would sound at his desk.

I pressed my thumb into the button. My other hand clenched into a fist.

I shouldn't be this hungry, I thought.

I had eaten the night before.

There was no reply. I slammed my thumb into the button again.

Nothing.

I was getting really frustrated now. I knew Stephen was at work. I'd seen his car in the lot when I pulled in.

Hunger made me desperate and volatile, and I pressed the button several more times in rapid succession.

"Stephen!" I yelled at the door.

As if my voice had summoned him, the callbox crackled. "Who is it?"

"Stephen! Open the door!" I demanded. I knew I sounded terrible. Deep hunger made my voice hoarse and my words hard to understand.

I heard the lock slide back with a buzz, and I pushed through the door roughly. I hurried down the hall and through the double doors that led to the examination room. Stephen was there, standing in the middle of the room with an electric bone saw. The body of a middle-aged man lay on the metal table before him, covered in a sheet.

"Hi, Del, I—" Stephen fell short when he looked at me. I knew I must have looked awful. "Fridge," he said.

I nodded and headed through the door that led to a small room directly off the examination room. It had a counter that ran the length of one wall. There was a half-full coffee pot, a printer, microwave, a small folding table, and the fridge.

My head was pounding as I ripped the refrigerator door open, my eyesight taking on the vivid and red-tinged perspective I called Zombie Vision.

Not very inventive. Sue me.

There was a Tupperware dish containing part of a brain inside. I snatched it up, grabbed a plastic fork from the cupboard because I was still presumably clutching to my humanity, and dug in.

Moving slowly, Stephen stepped into view. I hated it when he moved like that. It told me that no matter how well or long I knew him, he would always be afraid of me. It proved to me that to the people who knew the truth of my existence, I would always be a monster.

"You ate last night," he said.

It took me a moment to respond. "How very observant of you."

"My point is you shouldn't be hungry."

I shrugged and finished my meal. I didn't know what to tell him. "Maybe being angry makes it worse? This whole thing has me really rattled."

Stephen took the chair across from me. "If that's the case, then you need to really watch yourself."

I scowled. As if I didn't already know this. "I was a zombie for almost a year before we met. I can handle myself."

"Don't be bitchy," Stephen said flatly. "I'm just worried about you."

The buzzer sounded, echoing through the morgue. "Who the hell would that be?" Stephen said. He returned to the desk and pressed the callbox button. "Yes?"

"It's Detective Brookes again," said the voice through the speaker.

I sat up straighter, listening intently to the conversation. What was the likelihood of running into the same cop while in a rather suspicious location twice in one day?

"And how can I help you, Detective?" Stephen said.

"I had a message that you managed to get the toxicology report back."

As Stephen pressed the button to let Mike in, I realized he had no idea about my encounter with the detective earlier.

"Shit!" I hissed. How was I going to explain this?

Quietly, I stood and closed the break room door. The latch clicked just as the double doors to the morgue examination room swung open.

"Give me just a minute," Stephen was saying, "and I can print you a copy."

There was the sound of fingers on a keyboard, and the printer fired up *behind me*. I spun to face it.

Who the hell puts their printer in the break room?

"Let me go grab that," Stephen said.

"I can get it," Mike said.

I looked around the room but already knew there was no other exit.

"Shit."

Quickly, I threw the bloody Tupperware dish into the sink and ran some water over it, then sat back down at the table and did my best to look inconspicuous.

A moment later, the door opened, and Mike walked in. We locked eyes, and he froze in the doorway.

***

It was the woman from the theatre. Sitting at a table in the morgue break room. What was the likelihood of that?

Mike didn't believe in coincidence. Being a homicide detective made him question everything, and running into the same person at two different places where the victim had been on the same day was more than suspicious.

"What are you doing here?" Mike said after he composed himself.

"She came to have lunch with me," Stephen said before Del could answer. "This is my roommate, Del."

"We've met," Mike said flatly and strode over to collect the papers from the printer. "Apparently, she likes old theatres and crime scenes. Funny that your roommate would show up there after I came here this morning."

Stephen threw Del a confused look before painting perfect innocence across his face and shrugged. "She's a little eccentric."

Mike looked from Stephen to Del, who also shrugged. "You know, this is more than a little strange," he said, gauging her reaction.

"Probably," Del replied.

She didn't appear phased, and Mike made a mental note to look into this Del character when he got back to his desk. "Would you mind telling me where you were Friday night between 11 p.m. and 1 a.m.?" he asked.

"Asleep," Del said, a little shortly, and Mike got the impression she didn't like having to explain herself to anyone. "Stephen can corroborate."

***

Of course he thought I was a suspect. I sighed inwardly and prepared for more questions, but none came. For what it was worth, Mike seemed to believe me. He shuffled the papers before him and, seeming satisfied, said, "This is all I needed. Have a nice day."

He was gone.

Stephen waited until he heard the doors lock before blurting out, "What the hell was that all about?"

"When I went to the theatre earlier, he caught me."

"And he didn't arrest you? That's disturbing a crime scene. No wonder he was so suspicious when he got here."

"He doesn't seem like that much of an ass."

Stephen shrugged. "Maybe not. He hasn't been in Ogden very long."

"Do you know why he came here?"

"Nope, just that he's a transfer from somewhere back east."

"I see." Standing, I returned to the examination room.

"Are you going to go look for that bar?" Stephen asked.

"I was, but now I don't know. I think maybe I should just go home." I walked up the short flight of stairs and pushed through the door into the hallway.

"I'll see you at home, then?" Stephen called.

"Yeah. See you at home."

***

Mike sat at his desk, the darkness pressing in on the light from his lamp and computer screen. The desks around him had emptied hours ago, but Mike stayed, determined to find out more about Del Carter. He didn't find much.

She had a clean record, not even a speeding ticket. But her name appeared in five news articles over the past three years, all involving crime scenes and unsolved cases Del had managed to give key information on. In all of the articles, Mike noticed, she had refused to comment, and there had been no sign of activity in the past year.

There was, however, one interesting similarity between all the cases: all involved murders. Del had provided information about murders she should not have been able to know . . . unless she was the murderer. Or a psychic.

Mike looked at her photo in the article, hair in a bun, looking annoyed and embarrassed about all the attention. He decided, rather against his will, that she wasn't a killer.

He sat back in his chair and pinched the bridge of his nose. Looking at the clock on his computer screen, he saw it was close to two in the morning.

It was time to go home.

***

I lay awake, staring pointedly at the ceiling. The clock told me it was 2 a.m., but I didn't care. You don't have to care if you can't sleep when you're dead.

Truth be told, I was quite rattled. The sudden bout of hunger earlier caught me entirely unprepared, and I was unsure how to take it. I replayed the previous day in my head repeatedly, up until the moment when the hunger struck, but nothing sprang out at me as strange.

When Stephen came home, I had pretended not to hear him. I didn't want questions I had no answers to.

With an inhuman growl of zombie frustration, I snagged the remote control from the bedside table switched the T.V. on. By the time eight in the morning rolled around, I was well into season one of *Grace and Frankie* and had almost forgotten the previous day's mishaps.

My eyes fell on the clock, and I turned the T.V. off. I swung my legs out of bed and stood up.

"There ain't no rest for the wicked," I sang quietly, pulling my pants on. "And money don't grow on trees . . ."

***

Clara was flipping the sign that hung on the door of Paws and Claws from closed to open as I approached. She opened the door for me.

"Girl, ya look like shit," she said as I passed.

I snorted. Of course I looked like shit. I'm dead. But I didn't say that. Instead, I let the observation slide off my shoulders as I walked into the tiny break room. I dropped my purse on the nearest chair, and the bell above the door chimed. I could hear Clara greeting one of our bright and early customers.

". . . and please make sure you're the one that does it," the customer was saying in a prudish and nasally voice. "I don't like the look of that frotch assistant you've got."

"Of course, Mrs. Deveere," Clara said. "I'll take good care of Mister Schnookums."

Oh, Mrs. Deveere. I smiled grimly to myself. The Irish-hating English prude and her lovely Schnauzer sidekick, Mister Schnookums.

"Also, I want him clean, but don't give him a bath," Mrs. Deveere said shortly. "Mister Schnookums hates them, and if he comes home stressed again, I'm afraid I'm going to have to take him somewhere else."

I didn't hear Clara reply, so I braved a peek out of the break room. Big mistake. Mrs. Deveere caught sight of me and gave her abnormally long nose a great sniff. "Sulking around corners now,

44

are you?"

I stepped fully into view and shrugged. "I didn't want to interrupt you and Clara."

"I will be back for him at eleven sharp," Mrs. Deveere snorted, then turned and left the shop.

I looked at Clara. "The phrase 'we'll call you when he's ready' hasn't ever meant much to her, has it? This dog is a terror."

Clara got down on her knees so that she was face to face with the Schnauzer. "Del!" she exclaimed in mock surprise. "How could you say such a thing about Mister Schnookums?" She cupped his face and rubbed her nose against his. "The adorable Mister Schnookums! Yes, so adorable, such a handsome bugger, aren't you!"

Mister Schnookums just wagged his tail.

"You're going to make me sick," I said, and he growled at me. I stuck my tongue out at him as they passed on their way to the bathtub.

"Careful," I said, imitating Mrs. Deveere's voice. "If he comes home stressed again . . ."

"She won't," Clara said. "He hates everyone else." Then to the dog, "Don't you, Mister Schnookums!"

She was right. Mister Schnookums did hate everyone, with the exception of Clara and Mrs. Deveere herself. It was a fact I greatly resented because it meant that no matter how much Mrs. Deveere hated me, she would still be here every other Thursday at nine o'clock sharp.

The bell jingled again, and soon I was busy with the intake of customers as it turned into a very busy day. It wasn't long before I was soaked and covered in hair clippings, but I thoroughly enjoyed myself. With the bustle, it was impossible to worry about my zombie issues. I couldn't even find it in me to be annoyed when Mrs. Deveere arrived to collect Mister Schnookums and asked me if I was ever going to do something with my "disgusting mess of hair."

It was well past two before Clara and I had a dead space between clients and found ourselves alone in the shop.

"Well," Clara said, sounding a little winded, "that was fun."

I untied my apron and threw it onto the wet pile in the laundry room. "Yup. A few more days like this, and we can retire."

"Ha!" Clara bellowed. "I wish."

I was loading the washer when the doorbell jingled again. "Del!" Clara called out. "It's for you!"

My immediate thought was that Stephen must have stopped by, but I dismissed it. If it was Stephen, I would have heard him come banging through the door looking for me.

My next thought was that it was Michael Brookes. The thought made my stomach feel like I'd dropped a stone in it. He had probably decided my answers were less than satisfactory and had come to ask me some more. It's not like it would be difficult for a homicide detective to find my place of work.

"Did you hear me?" Clara said again.

"I'm coming!" I yelled, straightening up from the washer and looking at the door. Resigning myself to the fact it had to be the detective and that nobody else would be coming to see me, I left the laundry room and headed to the front.

It wasn't Michael Brookes.

It was Adrian Keller.

"Hi," he said.

Clara was beaming.

"Hi," I said, a bit flatly. I looked around the waiting room, but Clarence wasn't with him.

"I don't see Clarence," I said. "Did I mess up his groom?"

To my annoyance, Adrian chuckled, and out of my peripheral vision I saw Clara look to the ceiling and sigh.

"No," Adrian said, "his groom was as pristine as ever. I'm here to see you."

"Why?"

I was feeling really stupid now. Something that wasn't helped by the fact I was so ridiculously attracted to the man on the other side of the counter.

"I was thinking maybe we could try lunch," Adrian said in a smooth voice. "Clara has assured me that you have time."

I felt myself go pink.

"Err, well . . ." I looked at Clara, who was nodding at me. "Okay."

Adrian took me to a small hole-in-the-wall diner called Milly's Place a few blocks from Paws and Claws, where the people were friendly and the food was fantastic.

I ordered a burger and fries. Adrian got a salad. I made a mental note to be a good person and not judge his food choices.

"So, what do you do?" I asked him.

"A little of this, a little of that," he said. "Mostly, I work in security."

"What kind of security?"

He smirked slyly. "I'd tell you, but then I'd have to kill you."

I took a bite of burger and rolled the statement around in my mind. I was pretty sure he was flirting, but I really wouldn't know. I'm not good at flirting. In fact, I'm horrible at it. A subject change seemed to be in order. I was still trying to come up with one when Adrian asked me how I became a dog groomer.

The conversation went smoothly after that, and by the end I was pretty sure I had managed not to embarrass myself.

After eating, we argued over the check—a debate that went on for several minutes until Adrian finally relented and agreed to let me pay for my half, growling that he'd never let a woman pay for herself in his life.

"First time for everything," I said, smiling as I took the bill to the register.

Our waitress was friendly, brown-haired, and freckled. She was the kind of bubbly personality I could only take in small doses but didn't mind being around. She took my card and slid it through the reader, watching the screen.

"Sorry, dear, your card declined," she said sympathetically.

"Run it again, please."

My head started to spin. I'd been paid the day before, direct deposit and everything. I had *checked* yesterday. Behind me, I became horribly aware of Adrian watching the whole thing.

"It declined again," the waitress said and handed me my card.

"Del, I don't think that one is active yet," Adrian said with the grace of perfect improvisation. "Here, Maggie, try this one."

Maggie seemed about as taken with Adrian as I was. She swiped his card without question and handed him the receipt to sign as I turned what I was sure was a magnificent shade of magenta.

On the way back to the shop, I said, "I'm sorry."

"It could happen to anyone."

"I'll pay you back."

"I do not accept paybacks for dates," he said.

I missed a step.

Date?

Yes, I supposed it would have been considered a date—something I hadn't been on since becoming a member of the adoring undead. I was rusty. I didn't know how to *date*.

Not knowing what else to say, I said, "I need to talk to my bank. My card shouldn't have bounced like that."

"Would you like a ride there?" Adrian asked, as if helping me figure out my financial shortcomings was as common as taking out the trash. I should have been pleased. Flattered, even. Instead, it just made me surly.

"I'll handle it, thanks."

My words came out too short, but I didn't need him to take care of me.

We stopped outside the shop. "Thank you for lunch," I said and turned to go inside.

"Wait," Adrian said, "could I have your number? If I keep coming into the shop every time I want to talk to you, I'll look like your stalker."

A very handsome stalker, I thought to myself.

I dug around in my purse and produced a small notepad. I scribbled my cell number down and gave it to him before thanking him one last time and rushing inside. Embarrassment was burning my cheeks and forehead. I was positively mortified. Starting a new life in Mongolia would be easier than ever seeing Adrian again.

Clara was waiting behind the desk and pounced the moment I came through the door. "Well?" she demanded. "How'd it go?"

"My card bounced," I said glumly. "I need to go to the bank."

"I paid you," Clara said absently, clearly not interested in my financial status. "He made you pay? That ass."

"No!" I retorted angrily. "I argued with him, and he let me pay for myself, and then my card bounced and he had to pay. It was horrible."

I was frustrated and extremely embarrassed, which always had a way of making me angrier. I dug around in my purse for my keys, fuming. The more I thought about the date and my money, the madder I became.

Adrian only asked for my number out of courtesy, I thought as my hand closed around my keys, and I wrenched them from the depths of my purse. I was never going to hear from him again. I just knew it.

Watch him stop bringing Clarence because the date was a disaster.

My breath caught in my chest. I was never going to see Clarence again! I stormed out of Paws and Claws without saying goodbye to

Clara, my anger only growing as I stomped across the street to my bug.

Well, how did he think it was going to go? Springing it on me like that?

"Calm down, Deliverence!" I snarled at myself in the solitude of my car. I was being intolerable, even to myself. I was being one of those awful people like Mrs. Deveere. I was being a bitch. The biggest, brattiest, bitch. One step away from buying a Schnauzer and joining the Deveere Club.

I felt my lower lip pucker as I pulled into traffic, but I refused to let it go past that. I was going to go to the bank and handle things like the adult I was.

I'd get there, and they'd tell me "sorry for the inconvenience" and give me my money back. Everything was going to be fine, I thought optimistically.

When I got to the bank, I explained the situation to a teller and was directed to the desk of a personal banker. Her name was Meranda—a short, round, and pleasant-faced woman. She was very sympathetic, and I could immediately see why she was good at her job.

"We'll get this all cleared up for you, Miss Carter," Meranda said reassuringly. "I understand that must be very frustrating. Now, it looks here like someone decided to go shopping using your card in New York this morning. I'm assuming you haven't managed to teleport across the country, right?"

"No," I said. I wasn't in the mood for humor.

Meranda cleared her throat uncomfortably and continued. "I can have this reversed today, and you will receive your money back in five to ten business days."

"What do you mean five to ten business days?!" I blurted. All those positive thoughts I had worked so hard on where gone in an instant. "I'm broke!"

"I'm so sorry for the inconvenience," Meranda hurried on,

trying to hush me by speaking. "It's the best I can do. Five to ten business days is bank policy."

I stood, gathering my things. "Fine," I said darkly, scowling into my purse as I hunted for my keys and walked out of the bank.

I was still hunting for my keys when I got to my car. They weren't in my purse.

"Oh, shit."

I dumped the contents of my purse onto the hood of my car. Still no keys.

"Oh, shit!"

I stuffed the contents back where they belonged and tried the door handle. Locked. Trying not to throw a temper tantrum in a public parking lot, I squished my face against the driver's side window. No keys inside, either.

"Shit."

I sighed heavily and stuffed my hands into my jeans pockets, feeling defeated. There was a sharp, stabbing pain on the index finger of my right hand, and I jerked it out of my pocket. I held it up before my eyes and peered at the gash on my finger. A tiny droplet of blood fell and smacked against the pavement.

I had managed to cut myself with car keys.

My lower lip was doing the pucker thing again. I unlocked the car and jammed the keys into the ignition. The engine roared to life, and I pulled out of the parking lot going twice the speed limit.

I could go back to work, I reminded myself as I puttered along. There was always something I could be doing at Paws and Claws. But given my current mood, dog grooming didn't seem very appealing, and I had finished all of my scheduled clients.

I could go hunt down The Shack. I looked down at the dash and saw the needle on the gas gauge resting dangerously close to empty.

Scratch that.

With another heavy sigh, I turned down a side street and headed home, where I could mope in relative peace. I was ten minutes away when I pulled my phone from my purse and dialed my best friend.

"Missing me already?" Stephen chirped as he answered. "I'm flattered."

"Someone stole my money," I stammered into the phone.

"I'm sorry, love," Stephen replied gently. "It's going to be fine."

"And I went on a date with Adrian Keller, and my card bounced," I blithered on. I could feel the storm coming, the rush of frustrated emotions—the zombie pushing for control.

"He made you pay? That ass."

I paused as I considered the momentary déjà vu, then rushed on. "And the bank can't refund me my money for *five to ten* business days!" I paused here to take several deliberate and calming breaths.

There was silence on the other end of the line as Stephen waited to see if I was going to continue. Evidently deciding I was finished, he said, "Del, pull yourself together. Take a bath, have a drink, and I'll see you when I get home."

Since I'm a zombie, I don't drink on account that I worry I might eat someone. Stephen knows this, but it has never stopped his attempts to make me pick up the bottle.

Still, I said, "Okay. I'll see you at home."

The apartment building was as quiet as it usually was at this time of day when I arrived. I didn't bump into anyone on my way through the lobby and got into the elevator.

My deadbolt slid back with a *thump,* and I entered my apartment. Light was streaming in through the gap in the living room curtains, casting a pale sliver into the foyer ahead of me. Other than that, the apartment was dark and quiet. I didn't mind. I figured I could use some silence.

I dropped my purse in a heap on the small table beside the door and went into the kitchen. I flipped on the light and rummaged through the cabinets. Bowl, spoon, sugar, flour, other baking items. When I stress, I bake sugar cookies, and today felt like a day I could bake for all of Utah. I pulled open the fridge and found only a single stick of butter.

Okay, maybe not for *all* of Utah, but definitely for this tiny apartment.

I was rolling the cookie dough onto a flat sheet on the countertop when the vision hit me.

***

I was carrying a plate of cookies into my living room. The room was dim, lit only by a single lamp covered by a light-purple cloth. It cast the furniture in a lavender glow.

There was a single couch, a small recliner, and a coffee table. The coffee table held a crystal ball and a stack of Tarot cards. There was someone sitting on the couch, their face obscured by the shadows of the room.

"Do you like to bake?" he asked me as I set the plate on the coffee table.

***

I gasped as I was wrenched from the memory, shivering in my kitchen. I knew that voice. I'd heard it in a previous vision, yelling at Mindi when she awoke on the theatre stage. She knew her killer. He had even been in her apartment. But the vision ended before I could see his face.

Vigorously, I rubbed the backs of my arms and willed away the goosebumps. I continued my baking, laid the cookies out on the tray, and slid them into the oven. I puttered as I waited for the cookies, wiping down the countertops and washing the floors— generally perfecting the haven I could control. I'd just come inside from taking out the trash when the timer sounded.

Not bothering to wait for the cookies to cool, I took a particularly gooey one from the tray and popped it into my mouth.

Yuck!

I spat the cookie into the trash. It tasted horrible! Never before had my cookies failed such a test. Bewildered, I looked around the kitchen and spotted the culprit on the kitchen counter: the unopened sugar container. I had successfully made flour cookies.

My first thought was maybe I could remake them, then I remembered I had used the last stick of butter—which in turn reminded me I didn't have money to buy more.

"Damn it!" I yelled at the empty kitchen and threw the rest of the cookies away.

"I just wanted cookies! Is that too much to ask?" I demanded to know from no one in particular.

There was a knock at the door. I spun to the hallway but didn't move. I didn't want visitors! What kind of monster just shows up unannounced, anyway?

There was another series of knocks, more persistent than the first.

Haughtily, I marched out of the kitchen, down the hall, and wrenched the front door open.

It was Michael Brookes. He didn't look any better than the last time I had seen him. Same dark circles around his eyes, the shadow still on his chin. His hands hung to his sides, one of them clasping a manila folder. He was handsome in a disheveled kind of way.

"Well, shit," I said. I left the door open and proceeded back into the kitchen. I heard him step inside and close the door before following me.

"What can I do for you, Detective?" I asked shortly.

Mike surveyed my kitchen before speaking to me. "I want to know what you know about the Jane Doe case I'm working on."

"I don't know anything about it," I lied, folding my arms across my chest.

"I understand you don't trust me." He sighed. "But it really would be better if we didn't lie to each other."

He tossed the manila folder onto the dining table. Papers, notes, and photos spilled out. I recognized the faces immediately. I had eaten these people, and in turn I had helped to solve their murders. Mindi's photo was on top.

"I did a little digging on you," Mike said, drawing me back to the conversation. "Your name has popped up in five murder investigations in the past three years. Now you've become involved in a sixth."

I wasn't sure what he was getting at. "Have you come to arrest me?"

"No. I've come to ask for your help."

I stared at him as the silence stretched out between us. "Why?"

"Because I know you didn't commit any of those murders, but you helped to solve them. I don't know what you're involved in, but I need anything I can get at this point."

I motioned for him to take a seat, which he did, albeit grudgingly. I sat across from him and pushed the photograph of Mindi across the table.

"Her name is Mindi," I started, then waited while he pulled a notepad from his coat and started writing. "I didn't get a last name. She had a best friend named Jessica, and they were drinking together at some place called The Shack on the night she was killed."

I paused here and let Mike scribble away until he looked up at me expectantly.

"She was taken in a van," I said. "Her attacker was a man, and she knew him."

Mike stopped writing and looked up at me. "Knew him?"

"Yes. I think Mindi was involved in mild witchcraft or was possibly advertising as a psychic. She had a crystal ball in her living room, and a stack of tarot cards. Whoever killed her was in her living room, and she knew him."

"So you were in her living room?" Mike pressed.

"Not exactly."

"Go on."

"When Mindi was killed, a chemical was used to knock her out, but something went wrong. During the attack she . . ." I took a steadying breath as I recalled the horrific moment. ". . . she woke up and heard his voice. The man in her living room had the same voice."

"Did you see his face?" Mike persisted.

"No."

He finished writing and closed the notebook. "This is the part where you tell me how you know all of this."

"I have these . . . visions. They show me things, like glimpses into the lives of these people, first-person."

I watched him to gauge his reaction. I was a little disappointed in his utter lack of one. He sat across the table from me, silent in his contemplation, pale eyes fixed on me.

Finally, he said, "Okay."

"I know I must sound cr—" I began, then stopped.

"Okay" was not the response I had been expecting from him. It wasn't a response that fit into my "I know I must sound crazy" script.

"Okay?" I repeated. You know, just to make sure.

"Okay," Mike said again.

"That was not what I was expecting."

"Listen, Miss Carter—"

"Call me Del," I said automatically.

"Del," he corrected himself. "If this holds up, you've given me more information than I've managed to dig up in a week. Right now, I'm willing to roll with it." He stood. "So grab your purse and put your shoes on. We're going to The Shack."

"I'm kinda busy," I protested weakly.

He glanced around my obviously empty apartment. "With?"

"Listen, I'm having one hell of a day. I had a date with the dreamiest man I know, only to end up embarrassed when my card declined, found out I had all of my money stolen, and then came home and made flour cookies that were fucking disgusting."

I felt my lip start to stick out and bit it to hold it back.

"And I can't make any more cookies because I used the last stick of butter, and I don't have the money to buy more!"

Mike seemed unsettled by my sudden outburst, watching me the way you might a toddler—with a certain surprised, condescending, but not uncaring annoyance.

"It was my cookies," I said a little lamely. "They were bad."

"Del, I need your help. Please, come with me."

I looked around my kitchen, did an inward sigh, and grabbed my purse.

CHAPTER 5
THE INVESTIGATION OF
MINDI PARKER

The Shack turned out to be exactly what it claimed to be: a shack. I stood on the sidewalk outside the entry, wondering if I needed to update my tetanus shot before going in. This place was a standing infection.

When Mike and I set out looking for this particular dive, I knew from my Google search that there were two bars relatively near where Mindi had been found with the same name. We had a fifty-fifty shot and struck out at the first one. That landed us here.

Second time's the charm.

Mike got out of the car and stood beside me on the sidewalk. "Drinking here is like asking to get murdered," he said dryly.

I looked at him, trying to determine if he was trying to be funny. I didn't think he was, so I said, "That was a bit cynical."

"It was a joke."

"Well, fuck." This was going to be interesting.

The inside of the bar was dark and smoky. Smoking indoors in Utah is illegal, but that didn't seem to be stopping any of these people. The bar was just one large square with cheap folding tables and chairs near the door and two pool tables near the back. There was a single bathroom behind them. The door hung loosely from the bottom hinge and leaned against the wall, revealing a lovely commode and tiny sink inside.

Along the bar sat a half-dozen perilous stools against a backdrop of shelved liquor and an exceptionally flustered barkeep.

He was in his mid-forties and balding, an apron tied around his portly stomach, cussing as he cleaned up the glass shards from the bottle he'd just dropped. He didn't notice us come inside.

Mike sat down on a rickety stool and waited. I followed suit.

The bartender looked up at us, and without missing a beat, said, "IDs."

Mike pulled his badge from his pocket and dropped it on the counter. I placed my license next to it, and Mike's mouth turned into the smallest of smiles before it vanished back to wherever his dry sense of humor came from.

The bartender stilled at the sight of the badge and dumped the broken glass into a trashcan under the counter.

"What can I do for you, Detective?" he asked.

Mike pulled out the picture of Mindi and set it on the bar. "Her name is Mindi. She would have been in here a few days ago. Do you remember her?"

An expression of genuine sorrow crossed the man's face. "Shit. She's dead, isn't she? I told her that shit she was into was going to get her killed. Jessica's going to flip." He extended a hand to me and said, "Bill."

I shook it. "Del."

He introduced himself to Mike and handed me back my license.

"Her last name is Parker," Bill said. "Though I reckon you know that. She was a regular here. She and Jessica came in once or twice a week. Really nice girls."

"Define 'that shit,'" Mike pressed.

"Mindi was a psychic. I think she was the real deal, too. She knew things and could find things she shouldn't have been able to. Told me once to avoid the gas station by my house, and later that night, it got held up. She didn't even know there *was* a gas station by my house. She didn't know where I lived. Anyway, it's how she made her living, reading cards, finding things for people, communicating with lost loved ones. Mindi had a large client base that saw her, but she got a lot of whack jobs." Bill looked at the photo again. "Shit."

"Any in particular?" Mike asked.

"Mindi never said names, but someone broke into her house a few weeks back."

"Did she report the break-in?" Mike asked, pulling his notebook out of his pocket.

"I don't think so. I don't know much about it. Jessica could tell you more." He scribbled a number on a napkin. "That's her address."

"How do you have her address?" Mike asked suspiciously.

"She's my niece," Bill growled.

I cut between them before it could get nasty. "The night Mindi was here, did you see anyone following her, maybe watching her?"

"No. Go ask Jessica."

***

Jessica Peters lived in a small apartment three miles from The Shack in an old, squat duplex surrounded by rundown houses. Mike and I stood in front of apartment 304B. He rang the bell once, twice, then a third time.

"Maybe she's not home," I suggested.

"She's home."

"How do you know?"

"There's a car parked in her spot."

I turned around and realized he was right. A black Honda was parked in the stall marked 304B.

"Maybe she has two cars."

"You don't live in this neighborhood and have two cars."

Mike rang the bell again, then knocked on the door.

There was a rustling from within, and the door was opened by a petite woman in a short silk robe. Her eyes were bloodshot and her hair frazzled. I recognized her immediately as Jessica.

"What?" Her voice was thick with sleep.

"Jessica Peters?" Mike asked.

"Yeah. Who are you?"

Mike showed her his badge. "Detective Michael Brookes. I work in homicide. This is my associate, Del Carter. We have a few questions for you."

Jessica looked me up and down like she was seeing me for the first time, then shrugged and turned away from the door, leaving it open behind her. We followed her into a tiny living room, where we were offered seats on a frumpy old couch.

She disappeared into the kitchen and came back with a pot of coffee and three mugs. She poured us each a cup and settled into the recliner across from Mike. "Well?" she asked.

"When was the last time you saw Mindi Parker?" Mike said.

"We went out drinking a couple nights ago."

"Does she have any family?"

"No. What's this all about?"

"I'm sorry to have to tell you this," Mike said, "but Mindi Parker is dead."

Jessica sat frozen in her chair, the coffee mug nearly slipping from her hands. "Dead?" she whispered. "God, when she didn't call, I thought she was just busy. I mean, people have lives, don't they? I saw her just the other night. I *saw* her. How?"

"She was murdered," Mike said. "I'm the investigator for her case."

"Murdered?" Jessica said in stunned disbelief. "Why would someone kill Mindi? She was a good person! Are you sure it's her?"

"We have a positive ID."

I shifted uncomfortably in my chair. Jessica had no way of knowing I had been the one to ID Mindi, and Mike didn't know how I had done it—but as I sat there in the living room with Jessica, I was abruptly reminded that I had eaten her best friend.

Jessica was nodding as she placed her coffee mug on the table. She kept nodding as she sat back, trying to process the reality of her friend's death.

Mike broke the silence. "We have reason to believe that Mindi may have been involved in the occult. Is that true?"

"She was a psychic, if that's what you mean," Jessica said.

"Do you know of anyone who may have wanted to hurt her? Anyone who was angry with her?"

"Loads. Mindi was involved with some shady people. Crazy people who thought she would be able to tell them their future or put them in touch with God. Mindi always tried to avoid the zealots, but . . ." Jessica shrugged. A single tear rolled down her cheek.

Mike could sense Jessica was losing her grip on herself and hurried forward. "We were hoping to get an address, maybe be able to take a look around her house. We were told she had a break-in a while back."

The tears flowed down Jessica's face as she gave the address to Mike. "Someone did break in," she said. "They used her tarot cards to spell 'witch' on her bed. It really freaked Mindi out, but when she reported it, the police didn't take her seriously." She bit her lip and said, "I think you should go now."

Mike handed Jessica his card and said, "Call me if you think of anything else."

Her sobs could be heard as we left and closed the door behind us.

"So, off to Mindi's?" I asked as I slid into the passenger seat of Mike's car.

"No," he said. "I need to get a warrant. That way, if we find anything useful, it will be admissible."

Disappointment filled me. I wanted to go to Mindi's apartment. This had been an excellent distraction from wallowing. But I understood how important this was, and Mindi deserved justice.

"Well," I said, "damn."

"Let's go swing by Walmart, and then I'm taking you home," Mike said as he turned the engine over.

"Why Walmart?"

"Butter."

CHAPTER 6
ZOMBIES, VAMPIRES, AND KILLERS, OH MY!

Stephen was already home when I entered the apartment. He was in the kitchen, removing items from a paper grocery bag. He turned to look at me when I came in, garlic sauce in one hand and whiskey in the other.

"Hi!" he said. "I was thinking stir fry and booze."

"I'll take the stir fry," I said, dropping my purse on the table.

"Suit yourself." Stephen took a swig from the bottle, then pulled a wok from under the counter and started throwing thin strips of meat with garlic sauce into it. He was working the food over with a spatula when he asked, "Where have you been? I came home to find the cookie apocalypse."

I told him about the sugar cookies with no sugar and my adventure with Mike.

"It was nice of him to buy you butter," Stephen said, smirking.

I threw him a sideways glance. "It was just butter."

"Fun butter."

"God, you are *awful!*"

"I know," Stephen chirped, throwing veggies into the wok. "You'll never guess who called today."

"Your mom?"

Stephen's mother was one of those do-gooder Christians who was convinced Stephen's homosexuality could be cured by a proper relationship with God. That also meant she called *a lot* to check on him and to try to set him up with the latest single woman in her church group.

"Nope," Stephen said. "She's actually only called me twice this week. It was Carl."

"Really?" I was surprised. Stephen had a strict "one-and-done" rule with men. He said he wanted to stay a free spirit. I said he had commitment issues. "How did he get your number?"

Stephen shrugged. "Fuck if I know."

"What did he want?"

Stephen's spatula paused over the wok. "Another date."

"And you said . . . ?"

"No."

"You can't say no to everyone."

Stephen spun on me. "Usually, I don't have to, 'cause I don't give anyone my number. That way it takes care of it for me, 'cause they can never call and ask. Now someone got my number, and they *asked* me on a *date*. Like a *date* date. Not even a hookup date." He turned his attention back to the stir fry. "I don't do date dates."

"Was he a creeper?" I inquired.

"No."

"Does he live with his mother?"

"No."

"Does he have a job?"

"Yes."

"I think you should call him back."

Stephen dropped a plate piled with stir fry in front of me. "Add your brains and eat your stir fry."

I got the Tupperware container from the fridge and sprinkled frontal lobe bits onto my plate, mixing it in with everything else. "More Mindi Parker?" I asked.

"Yeah, but this is the last of it. Now that we have an ID, her body can be claimed." Stephen sat down across from me and dug in.

"So . . . about Carl . . ." I said.

He shook his fork at me. "No."

I sighed and let it go. Stephen's mind was set, and I wasn't going to act like his mother.

We ate in silence, but as the food on our plates began to dwindle, I struck up a conversation.

"I feel stuck."

Stephen shrugged, and I took that as a sign to continue.

"I can have these visions and tell Mike what I know, but I haven't seen the guy's face, and unless I have a miraculously specific vision soon, I'm going to be S.O.L. I'll run out of brains, and this guy is going to kill again."

"You're helping the best you can," Stephen assured me.

The doorbell rang. Two unexpected visitors on the same day. This might be the end of the world.

Stephen went to answer it. A moment later, he came tiptoeing back into the kitchen.

"It's Carl," he whispered. "Go tell him I'm not home."

"Really?" I asked incredulously.

Stephen made a rapid, flapping motion with his hands, mouthing *go, go, go!*

I rolled my eyes, pushed back from the table, and walked to the front door as Stephen darted into his bedroom. I checked the peephole and could see a short, handsome, muscular man with a Latino complexion standing in the hall. He looked to be in his late twenties. He had a single blue orchid in one hand and a copy of the *Lord of the Rings* trilogy, extended edition, in the other. Stephen would melt.

This was apparently Carl.

I opened the door. His dark eyes met mine, and we assessed each other for a moment.

Finally, he said, "I was wondering if Stephen was at home?" His voice was like velvet and held the faintest trace of a Spanish accent.

"I'm afraid not," I said. "Just missed him."

"Ah, what a shame. Would you mind giving him these from me?" Carl asked politely.

A chill ran through me, and the hair on the back of my neck and along my arms stood up as I watched him suspiciously.

Carl seemed to sense this, and he sighed. His movement was so fast I couldn't track it. One moment I was standing in my doorway, the next I was several feet down the hall, Carl holding my arm in a firm but non-threatening grip. I looked back to see my apartment door closed.

"Alright, listen," Carl whispered, releasing my arm. When he saw me eyeball the path back to my door, he added, "Please don't freak out."

"I don't have a lot of time," he continued. "If Santasia finds out I'm here, especially talking to you, this will be bad."

"What *are* you?" I demanded. "Who are you? Who the fuck is Santasia?"

Carl leaned back from me. "I'm a vampire. Santasia is my Coven Master."

"*What?!*" I exclaimed, staring at him in disbelief. This sounded like something out of a bad B movie, and Coven Master sounded like porn.

"Oh, c'mon," Carl said. "You didn't really think you were the only creepy-crawly in Utah, did you? You need to get out more."

I had never met another supernatural creature before, but I supposed if it was possible for me to exist, then it must be possible for Carl to be telling the truth. It would explain the incredible speed.

"You give me the creeps," I declared.

"Of course I do! You're a zombie! You have creepy-things radar!" Carl hissed. "I know this isn't going to be reassuring, but I try my damnedest to be decent, and I don't have any Hollywood vampire plans for Stephen. I genuinely like him, but he's pushing me out."

"He has commitment issues," I said before I could stop myself.

Carl nodded as if something had come together in his mind. "How about I offer you a deal?"

This sounded bad. Making a deal with a vampire had not been on my to-do list for the day, but my curiosity got the better of me. "What deal?"

"I know Stephen is home. I could hear you talking. I also heard you talking about the serial killer that has been stalking Ogden. I have the information of a Coven available to me. What if I let you know when I hear something about our neighborhood murderer?"

"In exchange for . . . ?"

"If you get me another date with Stephen."

"Setting him up with you doesn't exactly sound safe," I pointed out. "You could eat him."

Carl sighed. "Fucking Hollywood. Two things." He held up a finger. "One, vampires are not the ravenous bloodsuckers with no self-control movies make us out to be. It's not like *you're* something out of *The Walking Dead*."

He had a point.

"Second," Carl continued, putting up his other finger, "if I really wanted to eat Stephen, don't you think I would have done it when we hooked up?"

Another point.

I chewed on my lip as I rolled it around in my mind. "Fine." I finally said.

"Yes!" Carl gave the air a fist-pump. It seemed like a very strange thing for an emissary of the night to do. Tucking the movies into the crook of one arm, he pulled a piece of paper out of his jacket pocket and scribbled some numbers down on it.

"But I'm not promising anything," I hedged. "I can't make Stephen go out with you."

Carl nodded. "Nope, this is great! Here." He gave me the movies, orchid, and the piece of paper. "Will you give these to him?"

Before I could answer him, he was gone—the exact method of his disappearance a mystery to me.

I went back to the apartment with Stephen's gifts, contemplating how my small, strange world had just gotten a little larger with the addition of vampires, and wondered if I should tell Stephen about the exact nature of his one-time lover.

Stephen was peeking from behind his bedroom door when I found him. "Is he gone?"

"Yep," I said and handed him his gifts. "These are for you."

Stephen rolled the delicate stem of the orchid between his thumb and forefinger as he looked at the movies. "These are extended edition!" he blurted.

"Carl would love for you to call him," I said casually.

Stephen frowned. "He brought you to the dark side."

Oh, if only he knew.

"He seems like a really nice guy is all I'm saying."

"He went full-creeper mode on our apartment!" Stephen protested.

"Bringing you a flower and movies is not being a creeper. He's been here before. A creeper would be watching you from the fire escape."

"Maybe he is. We don't know."

I followed Stephen into the living room, where he dropped the movies on the coffee table. He fetched a vase with water from the kitchen and arranged the orchid next to the trilogy.

Stephen may not have wanted to admit it, but I could see he enjoyed the attention.

"What if I said it was important to me for you to call Carl back?" I asked.

"Why?"

"I want to see you happy."

It wasn't a lie. I did want to see him happy. But Stephen seemed to sense there was something else, for he caught me with a suspicious scowl. "That's very sweet and all, but you're bullshitting me."

"Not me! Scout's honor!" I held up my hand in salute.

Stephen was obviously not convinced.

"Fine. But you have to promise not to make any decisions or say anything until I am done explaining."

Stephen arched an eyebrow with a nod.

"Carl is a vampire."

"Fuck—" Stephen started, but I cut him off.

"You promised!"

When Stephen seemed like he was going to remain silent, I continued. "I am absolutely sure he is telling me the truth. I saw him do some spooky things in the hallway. He heard us talking about the serial killer, and he offered me information . . . *if* I would get him a date with you."

Stephen was quiet for several moments. He folded his arms and tapped his fingers on his bicep. "Okay."

"Okay?" I repeated.

"I'll go on a date with him, only because you need me to. But I swear to God, if you hook me up with another freaky anything, I'll . . ." He trailed off.

"You'll what?" I was smiling. Things were looking up.

"Oh, hell! I don't know! But it will suck," Stephen exclaimed and waltzed out of the room.

I shook the piece of paper with Carl's number at the doorway. "Do you want his number?" I called after him.

"He can call me!" Stephen yelled from down the hall.

I giggled, then pulled my phone from my pocket and sent a text to the number, giving Carl the okay to call Stephen.

His reply came quickly: *Fast work, Señorita.*

CHAPTER 7
PURGATORY

Now, there is something you should know about working in my industry. First, pet owners are by far the most difficult, from wanting you to read their minds to deciding they want something different done right in the middle of their dog's grooming. Second, I'm not a fan of Yorkies. Yorkies are the hardest dogs to groom, in my book. They come in a million different hairstyles, and most of them want to take your fingers off. Yorkies are by far the most talented breed when it comes to nailing you with a trio of urine, shit, and anal glands.

And that's where I found myself that morning. Hands deep in piss, shit, and anal glands.

Before me, standing defiantly in my bathtub, was a Yorkie. Her name was Coco, and she was a bitch. At a whopping six pounds, she didn't seem like much, but whenever Coco was on my schedule, I knew I was in for one hell of a time.

I squirted down the walls of my industrial tub and sprayed Coco—again. She had hit me with the Golden Combo already, so I figured it was probably safe to bathe her. I scrubbed, Coco tried to bite me, and after we were done, I put her in a kennel and turned a large industrial dryer on her.

I went into the laundry room for a clean shirt before fetching Sakima from the crates. Sakima was a 120-pound Great Dane, and I adored him. He was a regular, coming every two weeks for his bath and brush.

I was loading him into my tub when Clara cleared her throat behind me. She was shaping the face on a miniature poodle.

"So . . ." she said.

I watered down Sakima's coat and pumped shampoo into my hand, waiting.

"Stephen has a date," Clara said.

"Already?" I remarked. It was only last night that I'd had my intriguing encounter with Carl, which I now knew was short for Carlos.

"Yep. I guess they're goin' out to dinner tonight."

I made an incredulous expression that Clara couldn't see. Dinner? My stomach turned as I rubbed my hands on my pants.

Clara was still talking. "Carl is takin' Stephen to some fancy Italian place upstate."

I felt the knot in my bowels loosen. *Somewhere public, that's good,* I thought.

"I'm excited for him," I said. As I scrubbed, Sakima's big tail wagged furiously, whipping shampoo and water in great sweeping arches. As it is with all large dogs.

I could feel Clara's eyes on me, but I resisted the urge to face her.

"You could go on a date too, ya know," she said finally.

"The last one didn't go so well," I reminded her. "Adrian has my number, and he hasn't called. I think that says something about our date. I also haven't seen Clarence on my schedule in his usual two-week slot. I'll miss him. This goes to show you should never date clients."

"You haven't seen Clarence on your schedule because Adrian is a businessman who happens to be out of town," Clara said slyly.

That had me turning around. "One, why the hell would you bring up a date with him if you knew he was out of town? And two, how do you know that?"

"It seemed like an excellent segue after talkin' about Stephen. Clarence is boardin' at Sandra's Pet Motel. I'm friends with Sandra, so she let me know." Clara seemed completely unperturbed by the fact she had people spying on Adrian Keller.

"What are you? The CIA? Clara, you sound like a stalker."

She shrugged, and the bell over the front door jingled. We glanced over to see none other than Michael Brookes standing in our waiting room. I locked eyes with him, and he made a come-here motion with his hand.

"Who the hell is that?" Clara asked.

"Michael Brookes. He's a homicide detective."

"You kill somebody?"

"No!"

"Good." Clara nodded. "No way I could find another groomer on this short of notice."

I rolled my eyes, pushing through the swinging doors into the lobby where Mike was waiting, looking impatient and tired as always.

He held up a piece of paper. "I have the warrant."

"If you want me to go with you, you're going to have to wait. I have two more dogs to finish." I waved my hands to indicate Sakima in the back, inadvertently flipping soap suds onto the floor.

Mike and I stared at the puddle of suds before I gave a resigned sigh. The corners of Mike's lips tipped up ever so slightly before he walked to the benches, planted himself, and selected a magazine. I guessed that meant he was waiting.

I returned to my post, where Clara was now trimming feet. She held the foot in one hand, scissors in the other, poised in a way only practiced dog groomers could be.

"So what does he want?" she asked.

"He wants me to go throw my heebie-jeebie shit around an apartment for him."

Clara glanced at Mike and his magazine. "He's just waitin' around for you?"

"Apparently."

I got back to work but found it difficult to focus as I thought about Mindi and the warrant. I wanted to help, but my stomach also turned with the idea of what I might see. I drifted through the afternoon, doing my job well but without thought. When Sakima had gone home and Coco was finished, I snagged my purse from the break room and bid Clara goodbye.

Mike and I stepped into the thick Ogden air. Dark clouds were rolling over the city, promising rain.

Seems appropriate, I thought.

Mike was already in his car. He stuck his head out the window. "I already had to spend the past three hours waiting for you," he called.

I angled into the passenger seat. "No one made you sit there," I shot back.

He snorted, pulling into traffic. We'd gone about half a mile when Mike took a hard right onto a small side street and parked.

"Is this where Mindi lived?" I asked.

"No," Mike said as he got out of the car. "C'mon."

I got out of the car and followed Mike, who was already across the street approaching a squat brick building at a crispy clip. A small wooden sign over the entrance declared the building Mario's Fine Subs.

The inside was small, styled after a 50's diner with black-and-white tile across the floor. There were a handful of tables along one wall, and ahead of us, a long glass case. It was packed with people jostling for a position at the counter where a short Italian man and an army of what could only be relatives packed subs. The shop smelled like fresh-baked bread and spicy peppers.

I stood close to Mike's elbow, trying to avoid being bumped by too many people. I could feel the creature within bristle, like a dog raising its hackles. I shook my head to clear the sensation and took a deep breath of sub-laden air. It was delicious.

The man behind the counter spotted Mike and hollered cheerfully, "Mikey!"

"Hi, Mario!" Mike called back.

"Do you want your regular?" Mario yelled, already pulling down a loaf and starting on Mike's "regular" before he answered.

"Of course."

"What about your friend, huh?" Mario looked at me, regarding me from under bushy black brows.

Mike looked at me, and I shrugged. "I'll have to pass. The bank hasn't returned my money."

"She'll take one too," Mike said.

Mario prepared the two sandwiches, ringing us up ahead of others that had already been waiting, and handed us our sandwiches over the grumbling of many annoyed customers. Mario ignored them.

"You take care now, Mikey!" He looked at me. "And her too."

I pondered the peculiar statement as we shuffled out the door and back across the street. We settled into Mike's car with our subs and dug in. They were fantastic! After we were both halfway through our subs, we slowed down enough for conversation.

"Kind of convenient to be friends with the owner," I said.

"It has its perks," Mike replied through a mouthful of sandwich.

When our subs were finished and our paper wraps balled on the floor at our feet, Mike turned the engine over and started across town.

"So," I said, "do you have a family?"

I realized I really didn't know Mike very well. Not that it was terribly surprising. Our relationship had consisted entirely of dead people and suspicion.

Mike was quiet for a moment. "I have a sister in New York," he said finally.

"Parents?"

"No parents." He didn't elaborate, and I didn't press.

I hesitated, then asked, "Are you married?"

Mike's face tightened, his eyes growing hard and cold. It was gone as fast as it appeared, his cop face returning to his features. "No."

I chewed my lip, feeling embarrassed that I had touched on something sore. This conversation wasn't going very well, and I decided to drop it. We drove on in silence, and I watched the houses and shops roll by. After a while, we pulled into a small dirt parking lot in front of an old brick fourplex. We were only a few blocks from The Shack.

"Mindi's is the top right," Mike said, turning off the car and getting out quickly.

I was out right behind him, following him up the stairs to the door.

"Do you have a key?" I asked.

"The landlord is supposed to meet us here at five."

I checked my phone. 5:05. I blew out my cheeks and folded my arms. I'm not a patient person by nature, and murder made me more than a little antsy.

It was well past five by the time a small Mini Cooper pulled into the lot and a short fat man emerged from behind the wheel. It seemed to defy the laws of physics to have so much person come out of such a tiny car. He was already sweating from the effort. Beads of sweat clung to his dark upper lip as he reached the stairs and puffed his way up.

"You the cop?" he growled, his triple chin jiggling.

Mike flashed his badge. "Detective Michael Brookes."

"I'm Bentley," the man said as he produced a key from his pocket and jammed it into the lock. His huge ham hands concealed the key almost completely.

The door swung open into a dark living room. Bentley reached to the left of the doorway, and a sconce on the wall flooded the room with light.

"Have at it," he said. "I'll be in the car."

I barely heard him as I stared into the apartment. I vaguely heard Mike thank Bentley before he passed me and crossed the threshold. I remained where I was, rooted to the spot.

"Del?" Mike asked, looking curiously from me to the room. "Del?"

The apartment was filled with Minchkins. I had never seen so many. Dozens of small, dirty children with pale faces and blank, dark eyes. They slid like ripples over furniture and walls, crawling on all fours across the ceiling, little inky hand and footprints following them before they disappeared into the drywall. Some bore the distorted, stretched faces I had seen before as they slithered along, gobbling up the energy of the apartment.

Their sheer number shocked me. I had seen them here or there over the course of years. But now there were dozens crammed into the tiny living room. Their presence seemed to push against the walls with suffocating energy.

I had a flash of the vision I'd experienced several nights before, the taste of blood in my mouth. The way it felt to drown. I shuddered.

In the middle of it all, on the floor, curled into a fetal position of anguish, was Mindi Parker.

She wailed in silence, her grief beyond any realm I could hear, but her expression said enough. All around her, the Minchkins crawled, reveling in her pain.

It turned my stomach, watching them that way. Watching them wallow in the suffering of Mindi's soul.

In the few years I'd been a zombie, I rarely saw ghosts. It seemed a rarity that the souls of the dead chose to linger on our plane. I didn't know why, but I suspected it took something horrible to keep them here. Something soul-crushing.

Mindi's death had been just that. She had been ripped from this world by the hands of utter violence, by the touch of something evil, and her ghost suffered for it. I couldn't tell if she was aware of the Minchkins around her, but her pained eyes found me in the doorway and locked to mine.

She dragged me down into the depths of her sorrow, down into the pain of her passing until I was drowning in her death.

***

When I opened my eyes, it was dark all around me save for a pale light that shone over me and seemed to have no source. Stretching out in all directions was a great, black expanse, eating the light at the edges of my refuge. The floor beneath my feet seemed to be made of dark marble splashed by a thin layer of water. It rippled as I moved.

Fear gripped my stomach like a cold, writhing hand. My breath sounded loud and disruptive in this cold, dead place. Breath did not belong here; life had no place in the darkness.

"Hello?" I called out cautiously, afraid of what might hear me but also afraid of being alone.

The darkness around me shuddered at the sound of my voice

and drew back from it. Another circle of light appeared. In it was a room.

It took me several seconds to realize I was looking at Mindi's living room. It seemed warmer, somehow. Like the energy from Mindi's life there gave it some kind of glow. The furniture was less worn, the lighting softer. A gentle, lazy ripple meandered across the space, the energy of Mindi's home. This was the truth of her apartment. I was seeing it without the filter of reality.

But they were there too—the Minchkins. No longer childlike in appearance, the truth of them will be forever seared into my memory.

Short, lanky forms skittered about the living room. Pale, near translucent skin stretched too tightly across ghoul bodies; abyssal black eyes set above a great gaping mouth filled with hundreds of needle-sharp teeth; no nose, and only pinholes for ears. They moved about the scene like roaches, hungry mouths inhaling the energetic ripples.

I became suddenly aware of someone standing to my right. I started, nearly stumbling from my circle of light as I did.

Next to me stood Mindi Parker.

With some stark differences, of course. This Mindi was old—not old in the way that suggests frailty, but old as you would imagine a well-kept person would age. Her hair was shot through with white. Salt-and-pepper curls fell down to frame a creased face. Fine lines gathered at the corners of her eyes and around the edges of her lips.

Her body slumped forward subtly like a great weight rested upon her shoulders, and hands growing knobby at the knuckles clutched each other against her abdomen.

She wore the same light-blue dress I'd first seen her in, and as I looked upon her, I understood.

Mindi's soul was old. Gentle, but aged far past her mortal years.

I looked at her, and my stomach turned. Not from revulsion, but from sudden concern over what my soul would look like if it came under this kind of scrutiny. Looking down at myself, I looked the way I normally did. But maybe to her, I wouldn't.

What would it show? I wondered. What would I look like to her?

Mindi was watching me, her eyes calm, her expression pensive. I became incredibly self-conscious and took a great interest in my sneakers then, studying the dirty lacing.

Mindi clasped my shoulder, feeling as real to me as anyone ever had, and gave it an urgent shake. I looked up, confused. Her face had gone from pensive to distressed. She shook my shoulder with one hand, and with the other, she pointed.

I followed the direction of her knobby finger and realized her living room had gone eerily silent.

The Minchkins were watching us.

They stood utterly still. Lifeless. They didn't blink or seem to breathe.

Do they breathe? I wondered frantically.

Their eyes were alive, though. Dozens of wide, unblinking black eyes glittered as they watched us. Their mouths hung open, their lower jaws hanging down to their ribcages, tiny white teeth in clear view. They stood on everything: floor, couch, coffee table, the arms of the furniture. And they were staring right at me.

I didn't dare move as terror slowly gripped my heart and tightened my throat. I didn't know where I was or how I had gotten there. I was truly, deeply afraid of those ghoulish beasts.

They watched.

I didn't move.

After what felt like a life-age, the nearest Minchkin abruptly dropped its head to one side so that it lay flat against its shoulder. There was the audible pop of vertebrae, incredibly loud in the silent space.

The sudden noise caused me to give a slight start. It was only a minor jitter in my shoulders, but it was enough to trigger the Minchkins into action.

They surged toward me, a horrifying horde of grotesque bodies. Long-fingered hands and hooked toes propelled them across the dark space, saliva dripping from their gaping mouths.

I was too shocked to scream and found myself firmly rooted to the spot. I knew I should run. I knew I had to do *something*, but my body refused to act. It was like my mind had become separated from the rest of me.

Mindi grabbed me roughly by the shoulders and spun me to face her. She locked her gaze with mine, nodded once, and gave me a good, hard shove. I fell backward, expecting to hit the floor, but found only the void.

I was falling through crushing darkness, the silhouette of Mindi Parker above me for a brief moment before my view was flooded with Minchkins.

***

I had the painful sensation of slamming downwards, my body jarring with the impact, and my back arched painfully as the glaring light of the Utah sunset found my eyes. I was lying in the threshold just inside Mindi's apartment. Above me, Mike's face swam into view.

"Del!" he yelled, shaking my shoulders. "I'm calling the paramedics."

"No," I rasped, sitting up. "No paramedics."

The last thing I needed was for some human with a stethoscope and a blood pressure cuff checking me over. I would set off alarms all over the place, and when they realized it wasn't equipment error,

I would have some very uncomfortable questions to answer.

Mike must have seen something in my expression because he softened slightly, the hard lines of concern easing away from his face.

"You just collapsed. You stared into the apartment, and then you collapsed." He rubbed the back of his neck. "Jesus, you scared me. I couldn't feel a pulse or tell if you were breathing, and then right when I went to call the ambulance, you woke up."

I shifted uncomfortably, not looking at him. I wanted to explain, but there was no way for me to tell him he couldn't feel my pulse because I averaged three beats per minute. I knew because Stephen had checked. There wasn't a way for me to elaborate on being undead. So instead, I said, "I have a sugar imbalance."

Mike looked skeptical. "A sugar imbalance?"

"Yeah. I'm hypoglycemic," I muttered lamely, twisting around to look into the apartment. It was empty, quiet. There wasn't a single Minchkin inside, and neither was Mindi's ghost. I shuddered, releasing a shaky breath. "I have to be really careful with what I eat."

It wasn't a lie; I do have specific dietary needs. For starters, no more murder victims.

Mike stood and helped me to my feet. "Alright. I'll believe you, but if you pass out on me again, you're going to the hospital."

He stepped into the apartment, peering around the living room.

"Well," he said, "wander about. Throw your psychic whatever it is around and get me some information."

I followed him in, albeit hesitantly. The Minchkins were gone, but I could still feel them, like their presence in such vast numbers had stained the room. I could see them in my mind's eye, gaunt little bodies scattered about. A chill crawled up my spine, and I shook it away.

Mike didn't miss my shudder. "What?"

"There are nasty things here. Mindi's death has left some serious negative juju floating around."

I passed through the living room and into the kitchen behind it. The appliances and counter space were designed in an L along the wall to my right. To my left and against the wall were the washer and dryer. There was a small wooden table just to the left of the door near my thigh. Magazines and books on the occult were scattered across it.

One book in particular caught my eye. It was worn, well-read, and had several colored markers among the pages. The title read *Witches Among Us*. I reached out, playing my fingers across the binding.

His voice came to me, the voice I knew from my visions. From cookies and movie theatres.

"Those kinds of books are dangerous. They go against God."

They go against God?

Mike came up behind me, looking over my shoulder at the book.

"I have a question, and it could be a weird one," I said.

Mike came around to my side, arching an eyebrow. "Oh?"

"Were any of the murders religious?"

Mike thought about it for a minute. "My partner, Bruce, thought they might be. There was a pattern of dismemberment he felt reflects the 'see no evil, hear no evil, speak no evil.' The first woman had her eyes removed, the second her ears . . ."

"And Mindi lost her tongue," I cut in. "I think Bruce is on to something with this. I don't know how much help this will be, but I'm pretty sure I could recognize the killer's voice if I heard it."

"I can't take you all over the city listening to people," Mike said. "I need something more definitive."

I flipped the book over in my hands. "He was here. He saw this book, and he said, 'Those kinds of books are dangerous. They go against God.'"

"You said before that he knew Mindi. Do you think he could have been one of her regulars?"

"It's possible," I said, then something occurred to me. "But why would he come here if he's religious and believes it goes against God? It just seems strange."

"He's a serial killer." Mike shrugged. "They justify things in weird ways."

"But the key there is that they *justify* it." I dropped the book and rooted through the other books and magazines. "Maybe he targeted Mindi because of her involvement in this. Were any of the other women involved in the occult in any way?"

Mike stared at me. "I can't believe I didn't think about that. I don't know. We haven't looked into that. We really didn't have anything to make us think about it, other than Bruce's suspicion, until now." He whipped out his notebook, making several notes. "I'll look into it."

Mike took me home, speeding away to the bat cave once I was on the curb. I trotted up to my apartment, turned the key in the deadbolt, and let myself in. I was feeling pretty good about myself. I was helping. I was doing something with my undead curse.

My apartment was empty, and it took me a minute to remember that Stephen was on his date with Carl.

Carl, the vampire.

My life is fucking weird.

I dropped my purse on the floor as I folded onto the couch. I didn't realize I'd fallen asleep until Stephen plopped down heavily beside me, jolting me awake.

"Relax," he muttered sleepily. "It's just me."

His silk shirt was lightly wrinkled, tie loose, hair tussled. He leaned back against the couch so his head rested on the cushion behind him, chin pointing to the ceiling.

The living room was dark, the shadows of furniture barely visible. The digital clock on the entertainment center read 3:03 a.m.

I stretched but resigned myself to staying on the couch. Stephen apparently had the same idea, because he swung his legs around and draped them over my lap, kicking his shoes off onto the floor.

"How was the date?" I asked.

He didn't reply. His face was relaxed, chest rising and falling rhythmically as he slept.

My phone rang. I dug it out of my purse and recognized Carl's number. I flipped it open. "Hello?"

"Hi, *señorita*," Carl's voice rolled through the phone. "I have some information for you if you would like it. However, there is something you should know."

"What?" I demanded.

"I had to go through Santasia to get the information you need. My coveness says she would be happy to assist you, but you will owe her a favor of her choosing. I'm sorry, it was the only way I could get it. If I had known before, I would have told you."

I ground my teeth. I needed that information. Carl knew I needed it, and even though he sounded genuine, I couldn't help but feel slightly betrayed. I felt he had sold me out to this Santasia. Owing a favor to a vampire didn't sound like a very smart thing to do, and I would be a liar if I said I didn't think about scratching the whole thing.

However, there was someone in danger. I would never be able to live with myself if I ignored that.

"Fine," I spat through gritted teeth.

"If I were you," he said, "I would make my way over to an abandoned warehouse on 37th and Third, quickly."

He hung up.

Well, shit.

Doing my best not to jostle Stephen, I slid out from under his legs as quickly as I could, snagged my bag, and slipped out of the apartment. I hurried down to the parking lot, burning rubber as I tore out of the lot.

I dialed Mike's number as I drove, hoping I didn't pass a cop as I sped through town at three in the morning. His phone rang a half-dozen times and sent me to voicemail.

"Shit!" I snapped and dialed again.

This time he answered on the third ring, sleep coating his voice. "What?"

"I think that a murder is about to happen at a warehouse on 37th and Third," I blurted into the phone. "I'm heading there now."

Mike was instantly awake. "Oh no, you're not!" he barked into the phone. "I'm going to call this in, and you're going to go home and stay the hell away from there."

I hung up on him.

***

"Shit, shit, shit!" Mike yelled when the phone disconnected.

Del had hung up. She had *hung up.* She was going to go charging into a situation she couldn't possibly understand. It was *dangerous!*

Damn it!

He got out of bed in a scramble of bedsheets and scattered pillows, jamming his legs into a pair of jeans as soon as his feet hit the floor. He ran through his house, grabbing clothes and tying on shoes, his cell phone propped between his cheek and his shoulder as he called Dispatch.

Next, he called Bruce. The phone rang through to voicemail.

87

Mike swore.

He glanced at the clock: 3:15 a.m. It was almost ten minutes since Del's call. Assuming she had been speeding and ignoring most traffic laws, she could already be there. It would probably take another fifteen minutes for the cops to arrive, maybe ten if they were lucky. That left Del alone on this for at least ten minutes. Alone with a serial killer.

Mike didn't like the math.

He rang Bruce again but didn't bother to wait for voicemail this time. At that late hour, catching Bruce was going to be like catching smoke.

Mike grabbed his keys and tried calling Del again. No answer.

"Son of a bitch!" he snarled. What the hell was she thinking?

Mike roared out of his neighborhood, hurtling towards 37th. As he drove, he paused to consider his concern for Del. He hadn't been this worried about someone since . . .

He shook himself. "She is a civilian in danger," he said aloud. That was all it was. Del was a civilian, she was in danger, and it was his job to protect her.

That was all it was, really.

Mike nodded to himself. Nope, it couldn't be anything else.

***

What the hell was I thinking?

I knew the answer: I wasn't. There was someone in danger, and I was rushing blindly into the fray. My mind was whirling. I was probably on my way to interrupt a murder, I had pissed off my cop friend, and I now owed a favor to a vampire coven master.

"How do I get myself into these things?" I muttered to myself.

I was driving down Third, passing empty lots filled with trash and old buildings that had once been storefronts. As I approached

37th, a massive building loomed into view.

The warehouse sat on a lot of twisted asphalt and weeds. Tangles of them gripped two old cars that sat in the lot, long forgotten.

The metal siding had pulled away from the building in places, some of it missing entirely. What was left was covered in a hefty amount of graffiti. The streetlights around it had been destroyed, and the glass from their protective panes lay on the pavement below them.

I parked my car across the street and cut the engine, staring at the dark building.

It was huge. I had no idea how I was supposed to even *find* anyone in there, let alone stop a murder. I got a flashlight out of my glove box and stuffed it in my pocket. I took a deep breath, kicked my car door open, and stepped out into the night.

CHAPTER 8
THE WAREHOUSE

I approached the warehouse cautiously. It loomed over me in the night, blocking out the moon and casting me into a deeper shadow.

I stuck close to the wall to avoid being seen if someone was looking, and slinked around the outside, searching for a way in. I found it at the back of the warehouse, where the lower half of the back door had been smashed in. Torn metal curled inward, revealing the building within.

I crouched and peered into the gloom. As a zombie, my night vision is better than a normal person's, but not so much as to make looking in a pitch-black warehouse easy.

I could make out some silhouettes in the dark. Stacks of pallets, an old backhoe. Nothing that *looked* like the shadow of a raving lunatic.

I slipped inside, stopping at one side of the opening as I contemplated the flashlight. I disregarded it after a moment. Nothing like a blaring light as a dead giveaway. My eyes were adjusting to the heavy darkness, the details on the backhoe becoming more prominent as I approached it. Even the gentle whisper of my feet sounded loud in here.

I stopped again at the backhoe, trying to make out any doorways or stairs in the murk. I pressed my hands against the cold metal of the backhoe as I leaned around the edge, trying to hide as much as possible.

I sensed more than saw the thing on the backhoe. Raw instinct sent me somersaulting across the ground as whatever it was slammed into the cement where I had been. I heard the cracking of the floor coming apart as I whipped out my flashlight and spun.

I was alone.

My light played across the crater in the floor, empty. My zombie senses were running at full gear now, flared nostrils pulling in the scents of the warehouse, red light encasing the shapes inside. I was no longer encumbered by the darkness, but there was nothing to see.

Whatever had been on top of the backhoe was gone. I stared at the broken cement and shuddered.

A door was flung open to the side of me, pale white light cutting a swath through the black. The gunshot came right after.

The bullet ricocheted off the backhoe, burying itself deep in the floor beside me as I ran for cover. I shut off my flashlight and ducked behind a stack of pallets, peeking through the gaps.

A man stood in the doorway, tall and broad, the harsh light behind him hiding his features. His arm fell to his side, holding a gun. The room behind him looked like it had once been an office. What looked like the old remains of cubicles and desks had been shoved roughly against one wall, leaving a space clear in the center.

In that space created by the disregarded furniture was a woman. She was unconscious, her slack face turned toward me. My stomach turned as I recognized her.

It was the woman from my groom shop. The woman the little boy had been with. I had thought the Minchkin was following the boy, but apparently it had been following his mother.

The man turned abruptly and fled the warehouse out the way I had come. He passed by less than ten feet from me, but the shadows kept me from seeing his face. In hindsight, I supposed I could have caught him. I am a zombie, after all. But at the time, I was far too concerned about the woman in the room and whatever had attacked me.

I glanced around the warehouse, and when I saw nothing, I sprinted into the office, slamming the door shut behind me and bolting it. I dropped to my knees beside the woman, feeling for a pulse.

It was there, faintly. It fluttered against the tips of my fingers that I held under her jaw.

Blood was welling up on the side of her head, spilling down her face and matting her brunette hair. My stomach heaved as I realized she was missing an ear.

Hear no evil.

I leaped to my feet, looking around desperately for something to stop the bleeding.

Boards, wire, nails, and screws. I pulled open cupboards and drawers, tearing them free of their holds in my rush. Three drawers and two cupboards later, I found a roll of duct tape.

Duct tape fixes everything. Right?

As I turned back to face the woman, I noticed the doorway behind her. It was parallel to the one leading into the warehouse. I hadn't seen it before.

I crossed to it, braced myself, and ripped it open.

It was a bathroom. Tiny and in various states of disrepair. I tore the small vanity door clean from its hinges and found myself staring at a roll of toilet paper. The industrial kind that comes wrapped in its own paper. This one still had the paper on it.

Small favors.

I went back to the injured woman. I was wrapping her head in toilet paper and a protective layer of duct tape when Mike kicked in the door. His gun was drawn, held in a tactical position near his stomach—not the way they hold it up near their heads in movies.

He didn't look tired now. Instead, his face was set in grim determination, and his eyes were burning with rage. This wasn't the same man I knew; this was the homicide detective.

Detective Michael Brookes looked from me to the woman on the floor. Several police officers and a few paramedics flooded in behind him, and there was a frantic buzz of activity.

Pointing the gun at me, he said, "Deliverence Carter, you are under arrest. You have the right to remain silent."

CHAPTER 9
DRINKS IN THE SHOWER

I sat in the back of the patrol car. It had been at least three hours since I was arrested and walked out of the warehouse covered in blood, severely embarrassed. I had never had so many people watch me so viciously. In a moment, they were all convinced of my guilt.

There she goes, the maniac serial killer.

I protested the entire way to the car. I tried to explain what had happened. About the man, and the woman, and the duct tape. Mike remained stoic.

The woman was taken away by ambulance only minutes after Mike escorted me out. It sailed away in a blur of flashing lights and screaming sirens.

I was not only embarrassed, however. I was furious. I burned with rage. The plastic of the seat was cold at my back, but I felt like I was boiling. My eyesight flashed between a red haze and my normal sight as I scowled at the leather of the driver's side headrest behind its protective angle wire shield. I was determined to burn a hole through it with my vision.

Part of me understood Mike's motives. He had arrived to find me hovering over a nearly dead woman, covered in her blood after calling him in the middle of the night to tell him about a murder I shouldn't have known anything about.

Another and very large part of me wanted to eat him. Figuratively and literally. He had arrested me, the fucking asshole, after everything I'd done to help him. Mike had specifically told me before he didn't think I was the killer. Yet here I was.

Another hour passed, and the night was turning grey with the coming dawn when Mike approached the car. There was another man with him. He was tall and sported a crew cut, gesturing wildly in a way that suggested he disagreed with whatever it was Mike was doing. Mike placed a hand on the big man's chest, which brought him to a stop halfway to the car.

They spoke for a moment before the man glared at me and stalked back toward the crime scene.

Mike opened the driver's side door and slid in, closing it behind him.

We sat in silence for a while as I continued my fruitless attempts to light the headrest on fire via pyromancy.

"I know you didn't try to kill her," Mike finally said.

"Oh? Do tell." My voice was dripping with sarcasm and anger, and the top of his head that was in my view swam red. "I may be full of murderous tendencies you don't know about."

"Sarcasm would not be the greatest idea right now," Mike warned.

I laughed. "Helping you wasn't a great idea either, but here we are."

Mike sighed, his head rising and falling with the effort, and twisted in his seat to face me. I avoided his gaze, worried what my eyes might look like.

"The killer never leaves traces at the crime scenes, and you have an alibi for the most recent murder. You're telling the truth. You interrupted the murder," Mike said flatly.

"Then why arrest me?"

"I needed you out of the way. But now I need you to go home, get cleaned up, and come down to the station and make a statement."

Now I did look at him. "Am I free to go?"

He regarded me for a moment. "I really need that statement, Del. You are legally obligated. Please."

I said nothing.

Mike sighed again before exiting the car and opening the door for me. I brushed past him and got into my car without looking at him. I peeled rubber as I left the warehouse and Mike in my rearview mirror.

***

I arrived home a little after seven in the morning, storming up to my apartment in a fit of rage. I threw open the front door, startling Stephen, who was sitting on the couch in a silk kimono, one foot propped on the coffee table, painting his toenails. The slit in the drape was threatening to show me more of Stephen than I ever wanted to see, but I was too angry to give a damn. His hair was tied up in a baby-blue towel on the top of his head.

I stomped past him and into the bathroom, viciously scrubbing away the blood on my hands and arms with globs of antibacterial soap. Not that it mattered. There wasn't a disease in the world I could catch from it.

I climbed into the tub fully clothed, throwing my legs over the edge so my back was against the wall and my feet dangled over the floor. Violently, I kicked off my sneakers. One of them hit the vanity, and the other sailed into the hall.

I reached up and cranked the water on cold. I sat under it as it soaked through my clothes and into my hair. It splashed out onto the floor, droplets splattering me in the face as I sat brooding.

Stephen appeared in the doorway a moment later, looking concerned. Half the toes of his right foot were painted a brilliant orange.

"Do you want to talk about it?" he asked.

I shot him an angry look and continued my sulking.

Stephen arched an eyebrow at me, turned on his heel, and left.

I was instantly angry with him. How could he just *leave* me? Couldn't he see that beneath the smoldering zombie fury I needed him here?

My fuming was cut short when Stephen reappeared, a bottle of whiskey in one hand and two shot glasses in the other.

"There's only one thing that can make someone look like that," he said. "Men." And he climbed into the bathtub with me, silk Kimono included.

The stunt forced me to scoot farther under the water as he took a position identical to mine, though it looked far more cramped for a man his size. Stephen's toes brushed the bathroom floor. He placed the shot glasses in the tub on the other side of him where they would be relatively safe from the onslaught of freezing water and poured two drinks.

Stephen passed one to me. "Cheers."

He threw back the shot.

I turned mine upside down over the drain. "Cheers," I muttered.

Stephen watched the whiskey go with a plaintive sigh. "That's good stuff."

I passed the shot glass back to him. "I'm not a drinker."

"I thought maybe coming home covered in blood at seven in the morning after an obviously shitty night may have changed your mind," Stephen said. "Will you turn up the water? It's fucking cold."

I reached up and added hot water until the shower was a more tolerable temperature for someone who wasn't already dead.

"So," Stephen said after a moment, "would you like to talk about it now?"

I sighed and spent the better part of an hour telling him about the events of the past twenty-four. I didn't leave a single gory detail out. I even told him about the phantom attack.

When I finished, Stephen took another shot and said, "It's not every day you get to be arrested for murder."

I glared at him. "*Attempted* murder. Get out. I'm taking a shower."

"I thought that's what we were doing," Stephen smirked, and I elbowed him in the ribs. I kept elbowing him until he crawled out of the tub.

I pulled the curtain closed and began tossing my clothes over the rail. I heard Stephen knock the toilet lid down and settle onto it. There was the clink of glass as he poured himself another shot.

"You know it's seven in the morning," I said.

"What's the point of being able to legally drink if you can't legally drink whenever you want to?" Stephen threw back the shot and sighed. "So, what are you going to do?"

I sighed, squirting shampoo into my hair. "I don't want to think about it right now. Let's talk about Carl."

"You know, I was hoping attempted murder and boy problems would keep us away from this topic," Stephen replied.

"Well, I want to talk about *your* boy problems."

"It was good." Stephen sounded uncomfortable, the lid creaking as he shifted his weight.

"You don't sound convincing. Shitty sex?"

You know you're best friends when you're in the bathroom together as someone showers and the other talks about their date and the shitty sex they had.

"No. We didn't have sex. We didn't even kiss."

This was an oddity for Stephen. He was unabashed about his love of sex, and how well he used it to avoid commitment of any kind. I supposed if you're just "hooking up," no one asks about anything else.

I rinsed my hair and shut off the shower. "What's wrong with that?"

"Because he was so *classy*," Stephen blurted out.

There was a rustling around the bathroom, and a moment later, Stephen's hand shot into the shower, holding out a towel. I took it from him.

"He opened doors for me, drove, and paid the bill. He was entirely unperturbed by any looks we got. And he looked so *good*. Damn, Del! He's so hot!"

I wrapped the towel around myself and stepped out to face a fidgeting Stephen. I arched an eyebrow and waited.

"Then he brought me home, walked me to the door, told me he had a lovely time and would like to get together again, and he left!" Stephen said. "No asking to come in, no trying to anything. He just went."

He sighed and met my gaze. "It was too good. One date and I'm in trouble. I haven't felt this way since Mark."

He looked away from me quickly. Mark was a hard subject for him. He had been Stephen's boyfriend for almost six years before he was killed in a car accident. That was about a year before Stephen and I met. He rarely spoke of him, but I knew. Stephen had been madly in love. To hold something like that and then lose it . . . it damages a person. Since Mark, Stephen wanted companionship, but he didn't want love.

"One date is a little early to discuss the L-word," I said.

"I didn't say it's the L-word," Stephen replied with mock

curtness, "I said I'm in trouble." He stood and marched off for the kitchen. "I'm making eggs."

"With your clothes on this time, I hope!" I called after him.

CHAPTER 10
ALDON FRAYE

My statement was short, sweet, and to the point. I avoided having any kind of conversation with Mike before and after, and now I was striding across the parking lot toward my car. The building behind me was an old brick three-story with bars over the windows and cop cars scattered across the lot. The place had endured the test of time and hardy criminals, and as I walked away from it, I felt that was just where Mike belonged: In something solid and immovable.

During our interview, he had not made a single mention of my arrest or our disagreement. He called me only Miss Carter and was very direct and monotone in all his questions. He also let me know that I was explicitly banned from assisting with the case any further.

Cop Mike. I didn't like Cop Mike. Cop Mike and I were not friends.

I suppose it didn't help that I hadn't bothered to show up at the station until well after four o'clock. Mike told me I was legally obligated to make a statement. He just didn't tell me when.

But as I cruised home, I realized it was incredibly hard to stay mad at Mike. I liked him, and I knew he was doing his job, as much as I didn't like that. I was still mulling over this conundrum when I arrived at my apartment building and headed up.

I was a few feet from the door when I noticed it was open. The latch rested against the jamb, unlocked. I was immediately suspicious. Stephen would never leave the door open, and I hadn't seen his car in the lot. There was someone else in my apartment.

I should call the police, I thought as I approached the door.

I shouldn't go in there!

Caution warned me as I silently pushed the door open.

The foyer was dark, but I could hear the clanking of pans and the sizzling of things cooking. A delicious odor traveled down the hall from the kitchen.

The knot in my stomach loosened as I realized it had to be Stephen. No longer concerned, I stopped trying to be quiet and followed the smell of food.

I rounded the corner into the kitchen and came to an abrupt halt.

It wasn't Stephen.

In fact, I had no idea *who* it was. The man was turned away from me at the stove, an apron knotted at the small of his back. He was lean, built more like a runner than a weightlifter, white-blond hair pulled into a loose ponytail. From the back, he appeared to be wearing a Victorian-era suit, the small waistcoat and gathered sleeves clearly visible.

"Hello," he said, not looking at me.

I jolted. "Hi," I replied flatly. "What are you doing in my apartment?"

I still wasn't very worried. I am, after all, a zombie.

He lifted the pan from the stove with one delicate hand and faced me for the first time. I had no idea *what* he was, but I knew immediately he wasn't human. He was a little too *perfect* for that.

For one, he was far too pale, with an utter lack of imperfections and very fine, perfectly proportioned features. Modelesque beauty. A pair of shocking, large, emerald eyes watched me from behind thin-framed glasses. A fine silver chain dangled from them, getting lost in his sea of blond hair.

He was ethereal.

"I thought we should have a chat." His tone was light, and he smiled at me with a mouthful of sharp pointed teeth. He spoke with a mixed accent I couldn't place. It was like someone had taken several different countries and mashed them into a singular set of inflections, yet somehow, he made it sound proper.

"I don't eat dinner with strangers," I said bluntly.

"How tragic. How do you ever make friends?" His smile widened to a size that shouldn't have been physically possible, stretching up his cheeks. "How about this? I'll tell you a little about me, and you can tell me a little about you, and then we won't be strangers anymore!"

His eyes twinkled mischievously, and he still held the simmering pan in his hand.

"My name is Aldon Fraye," he said. "and I'm a grim reaper. Your turn."

I stared at him. Had he really just said grim reaper? In my three years of being a zombie, I had never bumped into anything like this, and that's saying something since I know ghosts, Minchkins, and vampires. I supposed it had to be possible that other things existed, considering I am a zombie, but I had never thought something as well known and *creepy* as the Grim Reaper could be real.

"You're the Grim Reaper?" I asked skeptically. Somehow, I had expected dark robes and maybe a scythe.

"No. I am *a* grim reaper. Not *the* Grim Reaper," Aldon corrected. "And now you owe me a question and *must* answer honestly. That is the way the Game is played."

Game? What game? I was quickly getting the feeling that the center of this man's attention was a very bad place to be.

"Now," chirped Aldon Fraye, "it's still your turn."

"My name is Deliverence Carter," I said, "and I'm a zombie."

"Oh, excellent! Plates?"

Aldon took a hot pad from a kitchen drawer without having to search for it and set the pan down upon it on the flimsy kitchen table. The oddity of the entire situation had me in a sort of trance as I gathered plates and silverware and laid them out on the table.

Aldon clapped his hands together as he surveyed my handiwork. "Oh, lovely! However, your forks and spoons need to be switched." He rearranged them before removing the apron and settled onto the chair across from me. His emerald eyes did one more sweep of the table. "Napkins?"

"Fresh out," I said. I was beginning to feel annoyed.

"Well, no matter!" He pulled a duo of handkerchiefs from his jacket pocket, placing one over his lap before offering the other to me. "Do sit, Miss Carter. I feel we have a great deal to talk about."

I accepted the handkerchief gingerly and took my seat.

Aldon served what appeared to be pasta with sausage and parmesan out of the pan, filling my plate before his own. Suddenly, he looked abashed. "Oh! It appears I have forgotten the wine. Excuse me."

The grim reaper stood from the table and moved to the refrigerator, pulling a bottle of white wine from the depths. He took a corkscrew from the silverware drawer and a pair of chilled wine glasses from the freezer. He placed one to the right of each of our plates and went to work with the corkscrew.

"I do hope you enjoy Moscato," Aldon said as he popped the cork from the bottle. He filled our glasses and set the open bottle beside the pan. "So," he continued, locking me with those piercing eyes, "you're annoying."

It was a flat statement, and he made it with the tone of a child who had once thought something interesting and now found it tedious.

"I'm afraid I don't know what you mean."

"Oh, I think you do. At first, it was rather fun to watch you, stumbling around, sticking your nose where it doesn't belong. But now you're foiling plans. You're in the way, and I just *can't* have that." He sipped his wine.

"This is about the murder I interrupted, isn't it?" It was more a comment than a question.

Aldon nodded. "I have come to tell you to politely to *butt out.*"

The phrase seemed strange, even comical, coming from the proper Mister Aldon Fraye.

"Why come talk to me at all? You're a grim reaper, why not just do away with me?"

He sighed as if I was boring him. "You aren't asking the interesting questions. An interesting question would be *why* I'm involved. An interesting question would be what the *plan* is. But no, all you care about is you." He took a bite of the pasta. "Mmm, next time it needs more salt. Anyways," he said, catching me with his brilliant eyes, "I can't just do away with you. That isn't how it works. I'm a grim reaper. I can't kill anyone who isn't on the List."

Aldon carried on before I could respond. "Since you are undead, you have already been on the List, and once you've been on the List, you can't be on it again." He took another bite and watched me, waiting.

Did that mean I couldn't die? Was this going to be my forever? The thought was too disturbing to visit at any length, so I focused instead on Aldon.

"But you're killing people," I protested.

"No," Aldon corrected me, "I'm not." He smiled maliciously,

needle teeth gleaming. "Are you ready for the interesting questions?"

"Fine. Why?"

Aldon clapped his hands together gleefully. "Boredom!" he proclaimed.

"Boredom?"

Aldon was nodding, his hair bouncing as his head bobbed. "It has been so incredibly boring. After the Black Plague, the Grim became a bureaucracy. Too many Grims killing the wrong people, hence the List. Now, it's just so terribly *dull*. Do you know how much it's slowed down since modern medicine?!" He slapped his hands on the table, watching me intently. His next words were a whisper. "They're even curing *cancer* now. Cancer!"

"So you're . . . *organizing* . . . deaths?"

It was coming to me now. Aldon wasn't killing people directly—he was arranging for their demise. It seemed a terribly thin line.

Aldon's grin was climbing to impossible height on his cheeks. "You have no idea what you can accomplish with a zealot."

"This serial killer, you have him thinking that he is following God's will?" I said in disbelief. "How?"

Aldon smirked and sipped his wine. "Thou shalt not suffer a witch to live," he replied.

"You have him convinced these women are witches? Why? Because they are involved in the occult? That's sick. You're sick."

Aldon shrugged. "Some would say so, but when you are as old as I am, I think you will have a different perspective."

"Isn't Christianity supposed to be about love?"

Aldon gave a bark of laughter. "Love? Have you read Genesis?"

I stared at him. I could feel the rage building up, tinting my vision red. When I spoke, my words rolled across gravel in my throat. My voice came out as a deep and violent rumble. "I am going to stop you. I am going to find this man, and I am going to stop this, one way or another. Now get the fuck out of my apartment!"

Aldon went eerily still, rich green eyes meeting mine. When he moved, it was like he was jumping from one space to another, like when a frame is cut out of a movie, causing it to jerk from frame to frame. It wasn't like the way Carl could move. Where with Carl there was a blur, this was a sudden step from one reality to the next.

Aldon snatched my jaw in one delicate hand, his fingers and thumb on either side of my chin, nails digging into my cheeks. The hand was like stone, cold and utterly immovable. I pulled back from him and got nowhere.

The beast shrieked within me. I felt it crawling up my spine and peering out of my eyes. "You attacked me in the warehouse."

Aldon met them without fear. His voice was steely calm. "I can't kill you, little beast, but I can arrange your death."

He squeezed. I felt my jaw fracture under the weight of his grip, but I stubbornly remained silent through the pain.

"This is something you may want to consider before you decide to take it upon yourself to get in my way again."

Aldon flicked his wrist, and the minuscule movement sent me spilling over the back of my chair. He stood and strode to the middle of my kitchen as I gathered myself up with a snarl and lunged for him.

A small smile played across his lips as he reached out into thin air and pulled forth a great black cloak. Its folds were like smoke; its hood a gaping void. Aldon twirled it around his shoulders, and as the misty fabric settled upon them, he blew me a kiss and vanished.

CHAPTER 11
THE KILLER

When I was a kid, I loved *The Avengers*. My love for this ragtag band of heroes has persisted well into adulthood, although my favorites have changed. As a young girl, I had absolutely loved Thor the most, with his funny way of speaking and epic hammer moves.

My least favorite was the Hulk. I never understood him. I just couldn't get my mind around it. Why was he always so angry? So violent? Why was Bruce Banner always so concerned about his big green other half's anger issues? Why couldn't they just get along? How did the Hulk not see how ridiculous he was being?

Those questions greatly affected my opinion of the Hulk.

They didn't now.

Now, I have my own "Hulk."

When the Other awakens inside, we go to war. It is a battle for the mind and body that I usually win. Now, here in my empty kitchen, the Other rose up inside of me. It clawed along my spine and raised the hair on the back of my neck and along my arms as I thought about those poor dead women. It brought my vision into sharp, red focus as I raged against Aldon's threats.

I stood there, shoulders heaving from my ragged breaths and the force of my anger, and promptly lost the war.

I spun and drove my fist through the nearest cupboard, ripping it clear of its hinges as I hurled it across the room. The table went next. I snatched it by one leg, twisted my hips, and pitched it into the opposite wall, dishes and all. It splintered against the washer upon impact. Plates exploded into shards of china. They pattered onto the linoleum, sparkling in the light.

Spilled wine lazily ran across the floor.

I watched it shining under the fluorescent lights and battled my way back to myself.

I took several heavy breaths to make sure my zombie urges had properly subsided. The waves of hunger and rage rose and fell, lessening like the tide until I felt like myself again and the beast slept.

Stephen walked in. I knew it was him because he entered with a "What the fuck?!"

I turned. "Hi."

Stephen was surveying the kitchen, mouth slightly open, eyes wide. They passed from the table, to me, to the cupboard, and back again. "You trashed the kitchen."

"I got upset."

"About?"

"I was attempting to tackle a grim reaper and I missed."

"The Grim Reaper? As in, soul claimer of the dead?" Stephen asked.

"*A* grim reaper," I corrected. "Apparently, there are a lot of them."

"I think it says something about out living situation when you tell me that and I am more concerned about the kitchen," Stephen said as he crossed to the dining room table and surveyed the damage. "What did he want?"

"To talk. I guess I'm getting in the way of his grand plans."

"Grand killing plans?" Stephen asked. "Well, the table is toast. I'll call the landlord tomorrow and see if he has any fixer-upper guy phone numbers. In the meantime, try not to destroy anything else."

"I'll do my best," I said. "The grim reaper is named Aldon, and apparently he has been organizing the serial killings. The killer thinks Aldon is God, and that he is on a mission to kill 'witches'," I explained.

Stephen shrugged. "Probably not the weirdest thing you have ever told me."

Sometimes, Stephen could shock me with his flexibility. He managed to be comfortable with his sexuality despite his devout Christian family and the fact his roommate was a zombie. He had just been told there was a grim reaper in his apartment, and his reply was a shrug.

"I suppose it's all the 'No witch should live' bullshit," he said. "But what is making this guy think these women are witches?"

"Mindi was a psychic. I think the others probably were too," I said.

Stephen nodded. "Well, I guess that means you're going to be next."

I stared at him. "What?"

"Aldon said you're getting in the way, and you definitely have the history for someone to think you're a psychic. Hell, even the cop you've been helping thinks you're a psychic. It wouldn't be hard to convince a serial killer who is hunting witches that you're a witch."

I thought this over briefly and decided he was right. "Cherry thought."

This was not going to end this way. I was not going to let that supernatural bastard scare me into staying home and staying out of it. And I definitely wasn't going to just wait around to get attacked, either.

I grabbed my purse, promised Stephen I would be careful, and stormed out the door.

***

I parked under Ogden Memorial Hospital twenty minutes later. I didn't care what Mike had told me—I was going to talk to the woman I'd found in the warehouse. She survived her attack, and maybe she had even seen her attacker. At least I hoped she had.

I shut the engine off and walked into the building. As I rode the elevator up, it occurred to me that I didn't know her name. I pulled my cellphone out and dialed Clara.

"Paws and Claws," she answered.

"Clara, I need a favor."

"Oh, Lord, here it comes."

"I need you to look up the woman's name who owned that little Pomeranian you groomed last week. The one with the little boy."

"Nicole Wilkins," Clara said, not having to look her up. "She's been coming for two years. Why? Is she okay?"

"I found her in a warehouse last night. She'd been attacked by the serial killer, but she's alive."

I swear I could feel Clara tense on the other end of the line. Hell hath no fury like Clara.

"That son of a bitch," she whispered coldly. "Del, I don't know how you get involved with this shit, but if you find this bastard, you make sure they catch him."

"I'm trying," I assured her, hiding my apprehension.

I hung up as the doors opened to the lobby, and I made my way to the information desk.

"I'm looking for Nicole Wilkins," I told the nurse behind the desk.

She arched a heavily penciled eyebrow, pursed deeply lined lips, and said, "Relation?"

"I'm her cousin," I lied, twisting my hands behind the desk where she couldn't see and keeping my face as convincing as I could.

The nurse hardly seemed convinced, but I heard the clacking of lacquered nails as she looked up the room number. "Room 333. Don't be long. Visitors are only permitted until six."

I nodded, speed-walking to the elevator and slamming my thumb into the UP arrow. I fidgeted while I waited, shifting from foot to foot as I watched the light above the heavy double doors.

The bell dinged and I hurried inside, pressing the 3 a little too aggressively.

More antsy feet as the elevator climbed to level three. I grumbled when it stopped on the second floor to let an elderly couple on, and I rushed off as soon as the doors opened to the next level. Reading the signs, I walked down a hallway to my right and stopped before room 333, heart in my throat.

This is stupid. This is stupid, stupid, stupid, the voice inside hissed.

I nodded outwardly in agreement and raised my hand to knock.

"Come in," said a woman's voice. She sounded weak and tired.

I entered slowly, peeking around the door before coming into the room.

Nicole Wilkins lay in the hospital bed, looking terribly pale even against the starch white of the bandage around her head. Her cheeks were hollow, and her eyes haunted.

Trauma does terrible things to people.

The room sported a small sitting area with a couch that could pull out into a twin bed. The boy from the groom shop was curled up on it, asleep. Beside him sat the Minchkin. She was perched on the edge of the mattress, back straight, tiny white hands pressed down on either side of her hips. She kicked her feet playfully as they dangled over the tiled floor.

I did my best to ignore her as I looked back at Nicole. She was watching me cautiously and spoke first. "Are you another reporter? I told them not to let any more reporters in here."

"No," I said, "I'm not a reporter. My name is Del Carter."

Nicole's eyes widened. "You found me," she whispered.

I nodded. I was twisting my hands again. "Um . . . I, uh . . . I was hoping . . ." I stopped here, trying to find the right words. "I was wondering if you can remember anything."

Nicole's face soured. "No. I already told everything to the cops."

"I'm sorry," I said quickly, "I'm not trying to upset you, really."

Nicole was looking at her son, asleep on the couch. "I will be forever grateful that you saved my life. I don't think you will ever understand how much, but I think you should leave now, Miss Carter."

I left Nicole's room feeling hurt and disappointed. I felt terrible that I had upset her and was still no closer to an answer. I stood in the hallway with my hand resting on the knob as I contemplated my next move. I knew immediately I didn't have one. This had been my entire plan and a shallow one. I had been hoping against hope that Nicole would be able to tell me something, *anything*, about the man that had attacked her.

I was so caught up in my thoughts that I didn't even notice the man until he was almost to me. I abruptly looked up at the sight of his shoes and straight into the eyes of the cop I had seen Mike arguing with outside the warehouse. He was a large man, towering over me in the hallway with his smoldering eyes and buzz cut.

"Can I help you?" I asked, my voice dry.

He flipped his badge out. "Detective Bruce Flanagan," he

growled. "What are you doing here?"

I didn't answer. I couldn't. His deep voice had splashed over me in a wave of recognition and cold anger. I could feel the Other stir and creep up my spine. I could feel Mindi's blood in my mouth, the taste of metal, the weight of a platter of cookies in my hands.

"Do you like to bake?"

I met his vicious gaze with the fury of my own, and he must have seen it there. He studied me through hardened eyes, and the dots were connecting inside his head.

I spoke, my voice cold and horrible. "Do you like to bake, Detective Flanagan?"

Understanding stiffened the detective, and he filled with rage. I could see it in his face, his eyes, his body. I could see the monster that had torn Mindi's tongue from her screaming mouth with his bare hands.

A nurse walked between us and into Nicole's room, breaking the trance. Suddenly, the realization of the situation I was in joined my fierce anger.

Nicole would be safe with the nurses. I hoped, anyway. I spun on my heel and walked off, careful not to appear to be hurrying. I pressed the button for the elevator but took the stairs, glancing back to make sure the detective wasn't following.

I pulled my phone from my purse and dialed Mike.

I should be calling the police! I thought as the phone rang. And tell them what? Their serial killer was a cop working the case, and I knew because I'd heard his voice in a vision?

Mike's phone rang through to voicemail, so I dialed again. I was on the fourth call when I reached the parking garage.

Voicemail.

"What the fuck, Mike?!" I hissed and dialed again.

Mike picked up on the third ring. "This had better be important."

114

"It's Bruce!" I yelled.

"What?" he exclaimed incredulously.

"Bruce is the fucking serial killer!" I shrieked. "I'm at the hospital and he—"

Something collided with the side of my head and sent me spiraling to the ground. The phone flew from my hand, breaking against the cement, but I could still hear Mike.

"Del! Del! What the fuck? De—!"

A boot crushed the phone. The glass popped like fireworks. Swinging casually beside it was the bloodied end of a baseball bat. The crimson and metal gleamed, rose, and my world went black.

***

The noises came first. A thud. Sounds of dragging. The creak of tightening ropes. Slowly, it dawned on me that *I* was the thing being dragged. Ropes gripped my wrists and ankles. My head was limp, chin resting against my chest.

My eyes fluttered open.

Seats, a stage.

They closed again.

Open, linoleum tiles, frayed red carpet. I began to suspect where I was. With great effort, I tilted my head back and looked up at the tattered projector screen. I was in the theatre where they had found Mindi Parker.

The fog was clearing, my body already healing from the wounds I'd received. My vision cleared. I gathered myself up and wrenched hard against the restraints.

Nothing but the groan of rope fibers.

A new sound joined in—the rat-a-tat-tat of well-manicured nails. I looked to the far end of the stage where Aldon sat. He was perched on the lip in his pristine Victorian suit, one leg dangling into space, the other crossed over it at the knee. He bared his rows of pointed teeth, grinning below sparkling green eyes. His nails drummed out a rhythm on the old wood.

"Oh, my dear," Aldon chided, "I told you to stay out of it. You couldn't even wait a *day*."

I looked around the theatre. "Where's Detective Flanagan?"

Aldon shrugged, lifting a hand to examine his nails. "Around."

I couldn't see behind me, and the old exit doors with their crooked signs stood empty to either side of the stage. He had to be there, though, somewhere.

I pulled against the ropes again and listened to the strain from the old armrests.

"It's no use," Flanagan said from directly behind me.

I heard the creak of the chair as he rose and came around to stand before me. He looked different now, less human. Monstrous. They say the eyes are the window to the soul, but when I looked at Flanagan, I felt the saying was wrong. His eyes were a window to an entirely different thing. A dark, cold madness.

Flanagan seemed at ease, his shoulders relaxed and his face calm. His gaze was almost serene as he stared at the long knife rolling between his fingers.

Soulless.

Aldon's smile had grown wider, more vicious. I realized Flanagan was oblivious to his presence.

"It wasn't supposed to be this way," Flanagan whispered.

I felt cold. An icy hand gripped my stomach. "What wasn't?" I asked, but I thought I already knew.

His quiet, dead eyes flicked to me and back to the knife. "Your death."

"You're going to kill me like you killed all those other innocent women?" I snarled.

Flanagan snorted. "Innocent women?" he said disgustedly.

"Hardly. I know what you really are. Beasts. Witches. Disciples of Satan himself."

We have officially crossed into Crazy Town, I thought.

"You think you're on a mission from God," I said. It wasn't a question. Aldon had already confirmed this for me.

Flanagan answered anyway. "My Lord has spoken to me. He has told me what must be done."

"Your 'lord' isn't a god," I snapped. "He's a beasty, just like you say I am! You've been played!"

In retrospect, yelling at a psychotic man with a knife was probably not the smartest thing I ever did.

The blade flashed. I felt the white-hot burn of steel slicing through my cheek, glancing off my teeth. Blood slipped down my face and filled my mouth. I felt the severed half flapping as it dropped beneath my chin.

The blade gleamed red as it bore down again with a wicked backhand. I tried to move away, but the ropes held me fast. The knife dug into the bone just below my eye, nearly blinding me.

Flanagan took a step back. "Speak No Evil," he announced triumphantly.

I felt the Other awaken inside of me, and when I looked up at that psychotic man, the zombie peered out of my ruined face. Red coated the theatre, outlining Flanagan in crimson light. Determination settled within me. I was going to kill him.

He watched me in shock, and the scent of his fear spurred me into a frenzy. I thrashed against the bindings that held me, screaming, spitting blood. It splattered my legs and the floor, sprinkling his boots.

He took several quick steps backward and bumped against the stage. He pulled his pistol from his waistband and trained it on me. The next few seconds happened very quickly.

There was a crash behind me as the door into the theatre was kicked in.

Mike's voice bellowed, "FREEZE!"

Aldon rose from the stage, transforming into something of nightmares. Great billowing folds encased him so only his pale face was visible. He rushed Mike, his teeth like daggers, his eyes blackened pits.

Mike, much to his credit, did not hesitate and fired several shots into the reaper. None of them harmed Aldon, of course, but he retreated nevertheless. Mike advanced into my field of vision, his face grim and set against the horror he faced.

I knew what was happening, what Aldon was trying to do, but I couldn't speak. The zombie had stolen my voice so all that came out were inhuman, guttural growls.

My mind flashed back to my kitchen and the conversation I'd had only a few hours before.

"I cannot kill you," Aldon had said.

Aldon leaped to the corner where the ceiling met the wall and stuck like a splatter of wet ink.

Bruce spun, taking aim.

"But I can arrange for your death."

Three shots rang out, sharp and deafening in such close proximity. Two caught Mike in the chest. A third cut into his thigh. He went down in a crumpled heap, his handsome face turned toward me. His pale eyes were cold, vacant.

I shrieked and heaved. The arms of the old chair snapped, no longer a match for me. The scream of twisted metal and my own furious cries alerted Flanagan, who turned to face me.

I felt the bullets more as pressure then as pain. Their force caused me to jerk violently, but they did nothing to halt my forward momentum. My thumbs went through Flanagan's eyes as I grabbed his head. His screams joined my snarls.

All the action movies show breaking necks like it is a very simple thing. Just a twist, and it's all over. It is hardly that easy. But for me, on this night, it was.

I wrenched Flanagan's head at a hard angle. There was the loud pop and grind of snapping bones, and he dropped like a sack of sand, silent.

I let him go and stood above his body as I fought the overwhelming urge to eat him. Finally, I shook myself and turned away. I didn't need to be haunted by his memories.

The corner Aldon had leaped to was vacant. There wasn't a sign of the reaper anywhere. I turned to Mike and was shocked and relieved to see him blink at me. He stared at me as though he was seeing me for the first time, and I suppose he was. Yet instead of the mild annoyance he often had when looking at me, there was shock in his eyes. Fear.

As we locked eyes, I could feel my cheeks stitching themselves back together. Watching the flesh of my battered face crawl back into place probably wasn't helping Mike. He lay framed in red light, and I knew that meant my eyes were flaming.

I must have been absolutely terrifying to look at.

Knowing this jarred me to mental clarity, and the tinge in my vision went out like a light. Pain washed over me like a cold splash.

As a zombie, I have a different perception of pain than I did when I was human. It's more of a deadened throb. The more severe the injury, the deeper the ache.

My torso was pulsing with the beat of my heart. I looked down at myself and understood why. Flanagan had hit me in the chest seven times in a tight cluster. I couldn't help but admire his marksmanship.

Gingerly, I reached around and felt my back, but my hand came away clean. The bullets were lodged in my body.

Mike stirred, struggling to get to his knees. I moved to help, but his hand shot up, gripping the pistol. "Stay back!" he hissed.

I froze. He made it to his knees, kicking his wounded leg out in front of him as his free hand unbuttoned his shirt. The Kevlar vest that had clearly saved his life was revealed.

Mike's breathing was ragged, but his aim didn't waver in the slightest. "Any second, SWAT is going to be coming through that door," he rasped. "Get out."

I didn't move. I didn't understand.

Mike jabbed the gun at me. "Get the fuck out. They see you, and they'll shoot you." He paused to take a breath. "I don't know *what* the *fuck* you are, but I doubt you want that kind of attention."

"You need help," I protested.

"Stay away from me," he snarled. The anger in his voice was cutting.

I flinched as though I'd been struck and stumbled out of the theatre, through the doors with their crooked exit signs, out into the night. A sob rolled up out of my chest. My eyes burned from the pressure of my tears as they cut tracks down my face and dripped off my chin.

Flanagan's eyeless face was burned into my mind, paired with the look on Mike's face as he stared in horror at me. They swam in and out of my mind's eye as they reminded me of the cold truth of my existence.

I was a monster. A beast.

I staggered down the street. When I was a few blocks away from the theatre, I sank onto the curb and buried my face in my hands.

I was alone, bloody, and hurt. I didn't have my phone. I'd left my purse on the front seat of my car, which I remembered with a wail was in the parking lot under Ogden Memorial Hospital.

A hand gripped my shoulder. I jerked my face upward and stared into the eyes of Mindi Parker. She was once again dressed in the light-blue summer dress, barefoot on the street. Her face held a small smile as she regarded me.

She cupped my cheeks in her hands. She felt as real to me as anyone. Her touch was gentle as she wiped the tears from my eyes. Slowly, she bent down and pressed her lips against my forehead.

A flood of peace washed over me. I closed my eyes and held onto the feeling with everything I had. Every part of my being gripped the sensation as it became my anchor in reality. Something fluttered against my face, and I opened my eyes to see a hummingbird in the space where Mindi had just been. It was a tiny thing, teal-bodied with deep-blue wings. I held up my hand, and she alighted on my finger before dissolving in a cloud of green and gold. It vanished before it touched the ground.

I let out a shuddering breath I didn't know I'd been holding and took stock of my surroundings for the first time. I had never been to this part of town before, but I had an approximation of where I was. It was several miles from home, but it was something.

I straightened up, gave my head a hard shake that I immediately regretted, and stood.

An hour of side streets and back yards later, I stood at the front door to my apartment, pounding my fist against it. Inside was the silence you would expect from an apartment at two in the morning, but I had seen Stephen's car in the lot.

I knocked again, slamming the side of my fist against the wood. If any of my neighbors came out to investigate the noise, this was going to be very hard to explain.

I heard swearing and stomping feet, and the door was ripped open by a blurry-eyed Stephen in a robe.

"Who the fuck—?" He stopped short, eyeing my face and the collection of bullet holes in my tattered shirt. "Rough night?" he asked and opened his arms to me.

I rushed into them, hitting his shoulder with a heaving sob. He guided me inside and closed the door, leading me into the kitchen.

"Stay right here," he said and went to the bathroom.

I stood in my demolished kitchen as I listened to the sounds of cupboards opening and closing. He returned a moment later with the duffle bag that housed our impressive first aid kit and an armful of towels. He dropped the bag with a thump and laid the towels out on the floor, directing me down onto them. He knelt beside me and started taking things out of the bag.

I saw the blood I'd transferred onto Stephen's robe and wailed, "Oh, Stephen! Your robe!"

"It'll wash," he replied calmly.

I looked at it skeptically. That was *not* washing out. But that didn't seem to bother him the slightest as he pulled hemostats, forceps, gauze, and bottles of hydrogen peroxide out of the bag.

"I need to see those holes," he said, hemostats in one hand and peroxide in the other.

I pulled my shirt over my head, unsnapped my bra, and hurled it across the kitchen where it landed on the overturned table. I lay topless on the floor, too exhausted to care about my nudity.

"Would you like a towel?" Stephen asked gently.

I shook my head.

He set about removing the bullets. He pulled the first one loose, dropping it on the floor. "Do you want to talk about it?"

I took a great, racking breath and felt a rattle in my lungs. Apparently, I had a puncture somewhere.

The words came pouring out of me, only slowing when Stephen removed a bullet. I told him about recognizing Detective Flanagan's voice, about the parking garage, and my tattered face. I told him about Aldon, about Mike, and finally, about killing Flanagan.

I swallowed and felt the tears coming again, running down my face. I had never killed anyone before, and even though I knew Flanagan was evil, it didn't make it any easier.

I looked at Stephen, who had been silent throughout my story.

He paused in his work to meet my gaze.

"I wanted to kill him," I whispered. "Thinking about Mindi, seeing Mike shot, I completely lost it. I *wanted* him dead, and once he was dead . . . I wanted to eat him."

My voice broke. I was appalled by my own words.

"Oh, God, Stephen! I wanted to eat him so bad!" I wiped my eyes and nose, feeling thoroughly sorry for myself and for all those poor dead women. "I'm a monster."

Stephen had returned to patching me up. "So," he said, "did you?"

"Did I what?"

"Eat him." Stephen pulled bullet number four out of my chest and glanced sideways at me.

I stopped crying, instantly sober. "No!" I snapped, rather indignantly.

"You could have," he said nonchalantly.

The anger was bubbling. "He was a fucking serial killer, Stephen."

"A monster wouldn't care."

My anger evaporated, and I was speechless.

"Del, you're not human, but I think the difference between humanity and monstrosity are our choices. Now, you're allowed to feel sorry for yourself. You've had a fucking shitty night, but don't unpack and live there. So you lay here and cry and bitch all you want, but don't you dare say you're a monster."

Stephen tugged on bullet number five until it came free of my body, then he splashed peroxide across my chest. White foam rolled over my skin, sizzling. The smell was disgusting.

I was silent through the rest of my home surgical procedure. Stephen patched me up and loaded me into the shower, pulling the curtain closed so I could strip the rest of the way in peace. I stood under the water for a long time, watching as it went from crimson to pink and finally ran clear. My hair was plastered against my body, but my skin was numb to it. Somewhere, deep in the recesses of my mind, I was aware the water was too hot, but I didn't care.

I sank to the floor and brought my knees up to my chest. I don't know how long I sat there, but eventually, I heard Stephen leave.

CHAPTER 12
AND SO A FRIENDSHIP ENDS

Days passed of me hiding in my room. Clara had been more than understanding, even though I didn't offer much of an explanation, but I knew I was going to have to return to work soon. I couldn't risk missing rent or losing clients.

No cops came to get me, which I found surprising. There wasn't a snowflake's chance in hell that I hadn't left evidence all over that theatre. So I counted my blessings and waited for the story to break on the news.

On the second day, it did—reporting the serial killer as dead, Mike as a valiant hero, and an unknown person of interest that I assumed was me. I felt a bit better knowing Mike hadn't ratted me out.

The thought of him hit me like a punch to the stomach.

Mike.

I called Stephen.

"Aloha," he said.

"Do you know where Mike is?"

"Do you really think that's a good idea?" Stephen asked carefully.

Actually, I knew it was a *terrible* idea.

"I need to know that he's okay."

There was an audible sigh on the other end of the line. "When he was shot, it broke three ribs. He's in the hospital, but he's stable. And Del," Stephen added, "be careful."

***

I sat in my bug in the parking garage of the Ogden Memorial Hospital. It felt incredibly surreal considering the last time I had been here I was attacked, beaten, and dragged to an abandoned theatre to be killed by a maniac who thought he was on a mission from God.

My hands wrung the steering wheel as I collected myself before I headed inside.

Nurse Pencil Brows told me where Mike's room was. This time, I told her I was a concerned friend, which was more or less the truth. She didn't need to know our friendship had probably ended a couple of days ago.

Mike's room turned out to be three doors down from Nicole Wilkins', which took me down the same hall where I'd confronted Detective Flanagan. Déjà vu had me nauseous as I approached the door of room 339, and I stopped short.

He doesn't want to see you, the little voice whispered.

I grimaced against it and knocked.

"Come in."

I entered, closing the door behind me.

Mike was sitting up, his bare chest pressure wrapped. His wounded leg was also sporting a blaring-white bandage and was elevated in a sling that hung down from a metal frame on the ceiling. Mike's face looked annoyed, covered in several days of beard, and he was battling with the T.V. remote.

"Fucking sports channels," he growled and looked at me. There were several tense beats of silence before he snapped, "Get out."

"I wanted to make sure you're alright," I said defensively.

"Well, I'm fine, 'kay? Now get out."

I shook my head. "You don't get to be an asshole just because you don't understand."

Mike rubbed his face with his hands, the effort stretching his cheeks downwards.

"You could have ratted me out," I said flatly.

He shot me a glare and sighed. "I thought that would be rude after you saved my life. I mean, you're the reason I got blasted in the first place, but still. And what the hell was I supposed to say, anyway? That I saw you rip apart a metal chair? Take six or seven bullets to the chest like it was nothing? Snap a man's neck? And then none of your DNA came up. Nothing. All 'sample mix errors.'"

His words were coming rapidly, like he was afraid if he didn't get it all out *right now,* it wouldn't come out at all.

"So I lied. I told them I didn't know, and it must have been the shock." He looked me up and down, taking in my lack of wounds and settling on my undamaged face. "Your cheeks . . ."

Mike trailed off, looking pale. The concern was gone in a moment, replaced by his Cop Face.

I shuffled my feet. "They weren't that bad. How did you find me, anyway?"

Mike snorted. "Bruce put you in his squad car. I figure he panicked when he grabbed you, because he wasn't planning it. All the cars have GPS. Your cheeks were hanging off your face. I watched one of them *crawl* back up. Jesus, Del, what *are* you?"

We locked eyes while I contemplated lying to him. Instead, the words, "You don't want to know," came out.

"Don't bullshit me, Del," Mike snapped.

"I'm a zombie," I said, surprised at my nonchalant tone. The words fell from my lips and pulled a great weight with them. As though by saying it out loud, I had made this whole thing more bearable.

He knows, I thought with an inward giggle.

Mike's expression was stony. He had seen too much not to believe me. "You're right," he said, "I didn't want to know. So you're a zombie. What was that other thing? The black thing?"

"That was Aldon," I said. "He's a grim reaper."

"The Grim Reaper? Named Aldon?" Mike asked incredulously.

I thought about pointing out it couldn't be all that strange for a grim reaper to have a name considering I, a zombie, had one. Instead, I said, "Not *the* Grim Reaper, *a* grim reaper. The Grim is a bureau."

Mike blinked, and the silence stretched on.

Finally, he spoke. "Alright, this is how this is going to go. You're going to keep your creepy shit over there, I'm going to keep my normal shit over here, and you're going to leave me the hell alone."

The words cut deep as I stood in stunned silence for what was apparently a breath too long. Mike gave a definitive nod, turned back to the T.V., and said, "Now get out."

***

I returned home feeling numb. I don't know what I expected from my visit with Mike, but it wasn't that.

You knew he didn't want to see you, I scolded myself mentally. *This really isn't that surprising.*

My thoughts were abruptly interrupted as I froze just shy of my door.

It was open. Resting against the jamb.

I nudged it gently, and it swung silently inward. I was greeted by the smells of sausage and grease.

This was the last thing I needed today. I stomped inside, down the hall, and into the kitchen, where I found none other than Mister Aldon Fraye.

He spun to face me as I stormed in, all glittering needle teeth and mischievous eyes. He wore an apron, and a frying pan was poised in one hand.

"Hello, Del," he chirped cheerily. "Let's have a chat."

ABOUT THE AUTHOR

M. Greenfield lives in Northern Utah with her husband and a menagerie of animals. She has been writing stories since she was six years old, and *Deliverence Carter* is her first published book. When she isn't writing, she enjoys martial arts, reading, art, and all things nerd. Visit her website at www.mgreenfieldbooks.com.

Made in the USA
Thornton, CO
07/13/22 09:08:52